MAGIC, MAYHEM, & A MARTINI

ANNA MCCLUSKEY

CHAPTER 1

Joan closed her eyes and inhaled the glorious aroma rising from her coffee mug, enjoying the rare quiet around her. She took a sip, savoring the bittersweet flavor. Opening her eyes again, she smiled as she surveyed her backyard. It was good to be home.

A sound came from the house behind her, and she sighed. When would her home return to the peaceful sanctuary she'd made for herself? It had been Curse HQ for almost a week now, and it seemed like every day another person moved in.

Joan turned as the back door opened, her lips curving at the sight of Brandon's rumpled dark hair and sleepy face. Here was one person she was glad to see.

"Hey, beautiful," he said. "I love you."

Her smile widened. She and Brandon had been on-again-off-again since they were fifteen, but this phrase was a new addition to their relationship, and she was planning to hold onto it. "I love you too."

Brandon plunked himself down in the chair beside her, and she nudged the second cup of coffee over to him.

"Oh, you're the best, babe," he groaned, picking it up and taking a long draft.

"Don't call me that," she said, automatically.

The door flew open again and Joan's best friend, Sadie bounded through it.

"What are you guys doing, lazing about? There's shit to do! Traps to set! Witches to capture! Curses to undo!"

"One trap. One witch. One curse," countered Joan. "There's time for coffee. Where are your spawn today?"

"I fobbed them off on Grandma," said Sadie, pacing around the patio. "I don't know what this witch-trap thing is that Wendy's got planned, but I figure it's probably not great for inquisitive pre-teens to be sniffing around it."

Sadie sneezed and reached into her pocket for a pack of tissues.

"Bless you," said Joan automatically.

"Thanks," said Sadie. "Damn fall allergies. Why can't I get them in the spring, like everyone else?"

"Why is that better?" Joan raised an eyebrow. "Don't you want to be unique and special?"

"I just feel like the cashier at Dimestore Drug judges me more when I buy Sudafed in the fall. Like the only possible use I could have for it is making meth."

"Who? Stephen?" Joan laughed. "He doesn't think you're cooking anything. He just hates you because you dumped his cousin."

"Who's his cousin?" Sadie frowned.

"Phil Smith," said Brandon. "He's still pining over you. Phil and Stephen come into the bar every weekend, and half the time it's just Phil talking about how much he misses you and Stephen telling him he can do better. For hours."

"That was two years ago and we dated for six months."

"The guy's got it bad," said Brandon.

Sadie tossed her chestnut hair. "Well, that sounds like his problem. He needs to get a damn life."

Joan's smile faded as the door opened once more and a flood of people came pouring out, busily arranging themselves around her table. Most of them she'd grown up with; they had been part of her first-grade class when their teacher had placed a curse on them and then disappeared.

Joan continued to sip her coffee, waiting until the whole group was seated – except for Sadie, who was more of a stand-and-fidget type. There weren't quite enough chairs anyway, and Finn ended up sitting on Veronica's lap. Finally, everyone was situated.

"I know we're all tired," she began. "I mean, I'm exhausted. I feel barely rested. But we have to move fast. Mrs. Olsen isn't going to sit around and wait. After seeing Ed yesterday – and him slipping through her fingers – she's going to be on a damn warpath, and we have to get her here, trap her, and convince her to lift the curse, or in a few months, we're going to be blind and mute forever, and our lives are just going to be absolute shit."

Sadie folded her arms and leaned back against the patio railing. "Great pep talk, Joanie! You sure know how to get people excited!"

Joan raised an eyebrow. "Oh, I didn't realize this was a pep talk. I'll try again." She took a deep breath, sat up straight, and pasted a strained smile across her face. She clapped her hands together. "Okay, team! We've totally got this! All we have to do is–" The teeny amount of pep she'd managed to muster fizzled and she slumped forward once more. "Nope. Can't do it. I am not a pep talker. Wendy? Just tell us your plan."

Wendy smiled brightly and straightened her spine.

Joan couldn't help but notice, beneath the confidence she exuded, some brand new bags under the witch's big brown eyes.

Wendy opened a green folder she'd brought out with her and pulled out a stack of papers. She handed it to Ed, who was sitting next to her. "Take one and pass them down, please."

Ed took a stapled packet from the top of the stack and handed the rest to Derek. "Wow. When did you have time to make these?"

"Last night. I couldn't sleep, so I put together a comprehensive plan. Joan, I took the liberty of using your printer. I hope you don't mind."

"I have a printer?" Joan accepted the stack of papers from Beth and passed it to Brandon. She glanced at her copy. It was quite thick, and the pages had been printed front and back.

"In the little nook off the kitchen." Wendy cocked her head, her brow furrowing slightly. "Buried under a lot of papers and a disused hamster cage."

"Oh, yeah, I think my dad left that here. He thought no printer was why I didn't print out my tax returns and make weekly meal plans."

"When did you have a hamster?" asked Sadie.

"You don't print out your tax returns?" Derek leaned forward, frowning at her. "What if you get audited?"

"You really should plan out your meals, sweetie," said Veronica. "You can't live on junk food forever."

Joan swung her head from one objection to the next. It was way too early for this."Um, the hamster was fifth grade, I think. I'll worry about an audit if it actually happens. And meal planning just makes me angry, and being angry every week can't be healthy."

"Wasn't that our class hamster?" Beth frowned at her.

Joan raised her hands defensively. "Hey, I didn't do anything to Mugsy. She was old, and she happened to die on my watch. That's it!"

"Why do you still have the cage?" asked Ed.

"I don't know! To hide my printer under? Why am I on trial here?"

"This is a very impressive document, Wendy," said Derek. He was already on page three. "Really well-put-together, well-thought-out…"

Wendy preened a little, running a hand through her raven hair. "Well, I like documents."

He smiled warmly. "So do I."

"I'm not super into them, myself," said Ed, flipping through his copy and then setting it down without reading. "Can you give us the gist?"

Wendy looked disappointed, so Joan picked hers up again to show support. After all, even though she and Wendy had gotten off to a rocky start, the more she got to know her, the more she liked the woman. Even if she had dated Brandon.

"The gist is that I've been going through my grimoire, and I think we have a real shot at catching her, disabling her, and then holding her until she agrees to undo your curse once and for all. But I'm not sure how to convince her. I do have some ideas outlined on page four." Wendy paused for everyone to flip to page four.

"There's no torture on here, is there?" said Veronica. "I'm not torturing anyone."

"You think I'd suggest waterboarding my own mother?" Wendy stared across the table.

Veronica shrugged. "I don't know. I just want to make sure my point of view is clear. No torture."

"And what are we going to do if none of these ideas work?" asked Beth. "Because I am not murdering her either."

Wendy's eyes widened, and she spun in her seat to face Beth. "What? No! What do you guys take me for?"

Ed shrugged. "I mean, we don't really know you."

"And you did kidnap me," Brandon pointed out.

"Not to mention plotting with the enemy and triggering our curse early," added Sadie.

Wendy's eyes darted around the table, her straight spine wilting slightly.

Joan spoke up. "Let's cut her a little slack, guys. She did reverse the early curse-triggering. And she was under a spell too. She wasn't plotting with the enemy – she was brainwashed and magically coerced."

"And I would never kill anyone," said Wendy, giving Joan a small, grateful smile.

"Well, good," said Beth. "Glad we're on the same page."

"And no torture?" Veronica raised her eyebrows.

"No torture either," said Wendy firmly. "Honestly, if you'll just turn to page four, you'll see – I think we can probably wear her down. She has very little patience, and she hates most people. Especially – how can I put this delicately? Anyone who might be a little bit eccentric."

"Excellent," said Derek. "So all of you can just be yourselves at her, and she'll be begging for mercy within a day."

"I'm not eccentric," said Veronica.

An awkward silence fell over the table. Joan stared at the pattern in the wrought-iron table in front of her, desperately holding in a snicker.

Derek cleared his throat. "My mistake. Meditating naked on someone else's back lawn is completely normal."

Veronica's perfectly symmetrical face split in an angelic smile. "Apology accepted, sweetie."

Joan flipped through her document, looking for page four, but page two caught her eye. "You seriously need all of these things for the spell? This is an insane list. Do you actually have this stuff? The spleen of a badger? Green-lipped mussels? Aren't mussels like clams? Do they even have lips?"

"Green-lipped mussels is an herb," said Wendy. "And no, I don't have any. That's a shopping list. The stuff I need from my house is on the next page."

Joan turned the page. "Holy crap! You actually keep this shit in your house? How do you sleep?"

Wendy shrugged. "You get used to it. How do you sleep with the cage of a murdered hamster in your pantry?"

"I told you, she died of natural causes!" Joan glowered.

"I feel like I remember something odd about it, though," said Beth. "Didn't the eighth-grade forensics club do an autopsy?"

"No." Sadie stepped forward to defend Joan. "They were going to, but they ran out of funding. The whole thing was just a smear campaign by that bitch Mandy Lessor from the school newspaper. Mugsy died of old age."

"Your elementary school had a forensics club?" Finn cocked their head. "With funding?"

"Not enough funding," said Derek.

"There was no need for an autopsy on Mugsy!" Joan growled.

"Okaaaaaay, moving on," said Wendy. "I'm sorry I brought it up."

"It's fine," said Joan, leaning back in her seat, her arms folded as she glared at Beth. "Let's just get this plan going."

Brandon nudged her. "Me and Joan can run up to Salem and grab this stuff from your place, Wendy, so you can get started on your set-up."

Joan sat up straight again. Some alone time with Brandon? Yes, please!

"Great!" Wendy said. "There's a key in the potted rosemary plant on the front porch. And then just go to The Broomstick around the corner and give the shopping list to the owner and she'll grab it for you." She glanced at Joan with a raised eyebrow.

"Just tread carefully around Diana. She's a bit prickly. And very powerful. You don't want to mess with those Council witches."

"Oh, that sounds ominous," said Sadie. "What's a 'Council witch?'""

Wendy shivered slightly. "Just don't piss her off, okay?"

Joan stood up, reaching for her coffee with one hand and Brandon's hand in the other. "We'll be polite. What could go wrong?"

CHAPTER 2

Joan stepped into Wendy's house and shook her head, amazed once again at the messy living room. It seemed particularly strange now, having gotten to know Wendy a little – she seemed so elegant and put together. Was this really the home of a woman who wore silk blouses and made super-organized eight-page (front and back) documents in a single night?

Every surface of the living room was covered in books, herbs, and oddities. She now knew, of course, that the oddities were spell ingredients and not just some kind of twisted decorating aesthetic. But you'd think they could be stored tidily or at least dusted off every once in a while.

"Seems like most of this stuff will be in the other room, right?" said Brandon, striding toward the arched doorway.

Joan followed him, surveying the rows of shelves in what would have been a dining room in anyone else's house. She consulted her list. "Okay, we need a bunch of skulls. Those are over there." She gestured toward a bookcase full of various animal heads – including a shelf that looked human. Luckily, 'human skull' wasn't on the list. "I hope they're labeled. I have no idea what a badger skull looks like."

Brandon picked up a skull at random, turning it over in his hands. "Yeah, it looks like they're tagged on the bottoms. This one is giraffe. Do we need that?"

"No. Badger, eagle, and wild horse."

As Brandon began picking up each skull to examine its label, Joan turned her attention to the next category – herbs. Most of them had weird names, like bloody dock, ashwagandha, and devil's claw. She wondered if Neo, the nerd with the bottomless backpack who had helped them out in Idaho, carried those around in his bag too, alongside the coriander and sage.

At least this room did seem to have some organization to it. Joan scanned the shelves of herb jars, noting that they were in alphabetical order. She pulled down jar after jar, stowing them in a black plastic crate from a stack in the corner of the room.

"Okay, I've got the skulls," said Brandon. "What's next? Entrails?"

"Worse," said Joan. "Eyeballs. Same animals."

"Ugh. Why?" Brandon moaned. He moved on to the next display case.

Joan finished up with the herbs and lugged the now-full tote over to the front door. Then she returned to help her boyfriend gather up some eyeballs because apparently that was what her life had become. Fortunately, the eyes were preserved in jars of formaldehyde, and not just rolling around on the shelf. They packed them carefully among the skulls, snagging some bubble wrap from a nearby desk.

"What's next?" Brandon asked, stepping back.

Joan consulted her list. "That's all for what Wendy already had on hand. Now we go to the shop around the corner."

"Sounds good." Brandon grabbed Joan's hand to lead her back to the car.

His hand was warm, and Joan's heart glowed, her lips curving in a small smile.

As they approached his car, Brandon dropped her hand, but the warmth lingered. Joan pulled open the passenger seat and slid in.

Brandon cleared his throat as he began to drive. "So, um, I've been meaning to ask you." He paused.

"Yes?" Joan's heart began to thump.

"About this whole love thing."

"Yeah?" She fidgeted nervously with her seat belt, running her thumb along the frayed edge. Was he going to take it back? He couldn't take it back. That wasn't fair.

"What does it mean?"

He was totally going to take it back.

"Mean? What are you asking, exactly?" she said nervously.

Brandon glanced over at her. "I mean, like, going forward. In our, uh, relationship or whatever?"

"I guess I hadn't–"

"Oh, hey, we're here." Brandon pulled into a small parking lot beside a two-story converted house with an inflatable witch dominating the front yard, complete with striped stockings and a broomstick. Wendy hadn't been kidding when she'd said it was just around the corner. But what had Brandon been thinking, starting a complicated conversation on a thirty-five-second car ride?

Joan trailed after Brandon into the shop, her mind going round and round in circles. Was he taking it back? Taking it to the next level? What did he mean by 'relationship *or whatever*'?

The shop looked much smaller on the inside than from the lot – just a single room filled with books and a counter in the back, behind which a handsome and imposing just-past-middle-aged woman sat, writing furiously in a notebook. The woman glanced up as the bell on the diamond-paned door announced their entrance.

"Yes?" called the shopkeeper with a frown. "Did you need something?"

Joan followed Brandon to the back of the shop. "You must be Diana."

The woman folded her arms raised her eyebrows, looking at him over her wirerimmed glasses. "Must I?"

Joan shrugged, a little taken aback. Then again, Wendy had said she'd be prickly. "I guess you can be whoever you want. I was told you'd be Diana."

"We've got a list," put in Brandon, sliding it over the counter toward her.

The woman relaxed slightly as she read it – the complete opposite of Joan's reaction when she had first laid eyes on this list. "Fair enough. I'll be right back. Feel free to peruse the books."

Joan never could resist books, but she found it difficult to really get interested. She just kept wondering what Brandon had been about to say in the car.

Anyway, as she glanced around the shop, she realized she already had most of these on her own shelves. They were just basics of Wiccan and druidic theory, with a smattering of quantum physics, and a few delving into unlocking psychic powers. All of these were topics that she and Brandon had studied in the course of their obsession with undoing their curse.

None of them had anything to do with actual witchcraft. So this part of the shop must be a front. Pretty clever, really – set yourself up as a witch store, only show the public what they think witchcraft is, and then keep all the good stuff in the back for your real customers.

Joan paused at a display of crystals. The theories circulating lately about the physics behind healing crystals were actually pretty fascinating, and she'd seen some interesting studies being done. She wondered if Veronica would be up for joining forces to conduct a study or two themselves, with herself as the physicist and Veronica as the healer.

Brandon stepped up beside her, picking up a large amethyst cluster and then setting it down again. "Hey, listen, Joan, can we continue our- Oh, shit!"

He grabbed her arm and shoved her behind a bookcase, following closely behind, shuffling her further back into hiding.

"What the–" she sputtered.

"Shhhh! Look!" Brandon whispered and pointed toward the door.

Joan saw a woman in a severe black dress, her figure distorted by the patterns in the door's glass, walking purposefully up the sidewalk.

The door opened and the woman walked in. She was older than last time she'd seen her, but Joan had her face etched into her mind.

It was Mrs. Olsen. Their first-grade teacher. The witch who had cursed them.

CHAPTER 3

"What is she doing here?" Joan hissed. "She's supposed to be in Idaho!"

Mrs. Olsen turned her head slightly toward them, and Joan slapped her hand over her mouth, ducking back behind the shelves. She locked terrified eyes with Brandon.

A *DING-DING-DING* rang out through the shop, and Joan and Brandon peered around the bookcase again. Mrs. Olsen now stood at the counter, craning her neck impatiently toward the curtained doorway through which the clerk had disappeared.

DING-DING-DING! Mrs. Olsen smacked the hemispheric bell thrice more.

Finally, Diana bustled through the curtain, an annoyed frown pasted across her face. She glanced up and froze, mid-step. As Joan watched, a parade of emotions raced across her visage – from annoyed to furious to calculating.

She carefully set down the brimming paper bag she carried and crossed her arms, her handsome face settling into a sweetly cruel smile. "Well, Marian Olsen. As I live and breathe. We haven't seen you around here in a very long time," she cooed, her voice full of honey, with just a soupçon of poison in the aftertaste.

Mrs. Olsen spoke, her deep, rich voice a bitter parody of her daughter, Wendy's. "Diana, darling. It has been too long. You look exhausted. Have the years been kind?"

"You are such a sweetheart to ask after me." Diana leaned forward against the back of the counter, resting her forearms on its wooden top. "And where have the years taken you? We've heard the rumors, of course, but I always said they couldn't be true. 'Marian Olsen doesn't have it in her,' I always said."

"Well, thank you, darling. I always knew I could count on Diana Peregrine to say just the thing. And your shop is looking as . . . quaint as ever." Mrs. Olsen gestured to the space behind her, and Joan and Brandon ducked undercover again.

"This could go on for a while," whispered Brandon. "It's just like when my mom starts talking to my Aunt Susan. They hate each other."

"We can't leave, though," Joan whispered back. "What about our stuff? If she's already in town, we're going to need it even more, before she finds us."

"Well, thank you, sweetheart. It's as well-stocked as ever too. Did you need something for one of your little magical doodles? I do keep a few novice items in the back," said Diana.

"Oh, burn," whispered Joan.

"I'm sure that comes in handy for you and your daughter," Mrs. Olsen cooed. "Carrie must be all grown up now, I'm sure. Has she managed to move beyond levitation spells yet?"

"Carrie is working for one of my colleagues on the Council of Matriarchs now, actually." A certain smugness entered Diana's voice. "And do you really want to talk daughters, Marian? When did you last see yours? Thirty years ago? Is she a good little mage now?"

Joan heard a strange hissing sound and peeked around the bookcase again. Her eyes widened when she realized that the sound was coming from Mrs. Olsen.

Mrs. Olsen clamped her lips and the sound stopped. She visibly collected herself, staring into Diana's smirking face. "My daughter is a witch, through and through. And I've got big plans for her. You'll see. You'll all see. Your Council of Matriarchs is a joke, and Wendy is bound for greater things than huddling in a chamber, cowering from the outside world, imposing rule after rule upon witches just trying to live their best lives. We'll show you. We'll show you all."

Diana cocked her head, looking thoughtful as she studied Mrs. Olsen's face. "That's right, your daughter's name is Wendy. She doesn't use your last name, though, does she?"

"She will."

Suddenly, Diana was all business. "I'm sure she will absolutely come around. Did you need any supplies today, Marian? I'm happy to gather them for you."

Mrs. Olsen narrowed her eyes. "Yes. Here is my list." She thrust a yellow legal pad toward Diana, who took it from her. "I'll be back for these later."

Mrs. Olsen spun on her heel and marched out of the shop, slamming the door behind her, the bell clanging as it shook and spun wildly.

Joan and Brandon stared after her and then looked at each other again. As Joan opened her mouth to suggest that they could get their own goods now, Brandon jumped backward. Joan turned her head to look over her shoulder.

Diana was suddenly standing very close behind her. Joan spun around, backing into Brandon.

The witch smiled sweetly and addressed Brandon. "I know where I've seen you before."

"Oh, um, where?"

"You're Wendy Sharp's friend. And Wendy Sharp is Marian Olsen's daughter, isn't she?"

"Yeah, what about it?" demanded Joan.

"The rumors are true, aren't they?" Diana said, satisfaction filling her voice.

"What rumors?" said Brandon.

"Thirty years ago, she cursed a bunch of kids down in Alexandria. That's why she disappeared. And I bet you're two of them. You hid when she came in. The question is, what are you doing about it? And whose side is Wendy on?"

"Whose side are you on?" countered Joan.

Diana studied Joan for a long moment.

Joan glared back. She'd faced down Wendy, back when they'd been on opposing sides, and she could face down this witch too. Although this witch was probably better at magic and more experienced than Wendy.

'Very powerful', Wendy had said. *'You don't want to mess with those Council witches.'*

Her resolve faltered a little, but she kept her gaze steady and lifted her chin.

"I am on the side of the Council of Matriarchs," Diana finally responded. "And we do frown on curses being placed on non-magical children."

"You mean it's okay to put curses on kids, as long as they're magical kids?" said Brandon.

Diana shrugged. "Depends on the circumstances. But Marian needs to learn that there are consequences for waving witchcraft out in the open where anyone can see it."

"So you'll help us?" Joan asked.

"Maybe." Diana turned away, striding back to her counter.

Joan and Brandon trailed after her.

"Maybe? Why wouldn't you? We're the enemy of your enemy, right? So that makes you our proverbial friend," Joan pointed out.

Diana rolled her eyes. "I'm not interested in clichés, honey."

"Don't call me that."

Diana spun around and leaned across the counter again, catching Joan in her piercing gaze, her green eyes staring deep into Joan's blue ones. "You are an ordinary, powerless little girl, and I will call you whatever I please, and I will help you or not, as I please."

Fury filled Joanin a wave, starting with her gut and raging upward as she struggled to move her head. Realizing that the power that held her came from Diana's eyes, she closed her own and felt the vise release immediately. She snapped her eyes back open and lunged over the counter, arms reaching for the witch.

Brandon grabbed her waist, holding her back.

Diana laughed, clapping her hands. "Impressive! You may be powerless, but you're smart. You don't need my help – Marian Olsen is a nothing but a pathetic, bitter old woman." She tapped a scarlet manicured nail against her lips and then shook her head with finality. "And I would like to see how young Wendy handles the situation." She glanced into the paper bag she'd brought from the back room. "Based on these supplies, I'm guessing she's going to try and trap Marian in Shaddell's Box, yes?"

"I don't know," Joan snarled, shaking off Brandon's hands. "I'm just the powerless little errand girl."

Diana nodded. "That seems likely. Yes, I want to see how this plays out. But the supplies are on me. Call it my contribution to your cause." She pushed the bag across the countertop.

Joan crossed her arms, glaring at Diana. "We didn't need any help anyway. We can handle ourselves."

"Sure you can, honey." Diana smiled smugly.

"Come on." Brandon grabbed the sack and dragged Joan out of the shop by her arm. "Thank you for the stuff," he called over his shoulder.

Joan turned back and gave Diana the finger.

Diana's grin widened.

Chapter 4

"Well, that was productive," said Brandon starting his car.

Joan twisted in her seat to glare at him. "What did you want me to do? Beg and plead with her to help out us poor little mortals?"

"I guess not," he said. "But did you have to piss her off? She seems like kind of a bad-ass. And Wendy told us to tread carefully around her."

"Screw her. She pissed me off first."

Brandon glanced over at her as he turned out of the parking lot, a small smile tugging at the corners of his lips. "You did hold your own, though. That was pretty fantastic."

"I know, right?" She grinned.

Brandon reached over to squeeze her leg. "You're a bad-ass too. I love you, babe."

"Mmm. Love you too."

They drove in companionable quiet for a while. Joan spent the time thinking about all the ways in which this whole scrappy-ordinary-people-and-half-trained-witch-set-trap-for-experienced-magic-user situation could go terribly awry.

Brandon broke the silence abruptly. "Listen, about what we were saying before." He paused.

Oh, yeah. This again. "Just spit it out!" Joan closed her eyes, bracing herself for the worst, her whole body tensing up.

"Yeah, sorry. I just wanted to say that after all of this curse shit is over, I want us to have a life. Together. Are we on the same page?"

"Yes!" Joan breathed a sigh of relief, her eyes popping open, her tension draining. "I'm so glad you said that. I was afraid you wanted to take it back or something."

"Take it back? I've been wanting to say that to you for ages, but I was never really sure you felt the same way," he admitted, resting his hand on her thigh again.

"I guess I did. I never really thought it through in quite that way." Joan grinned and laid her own hand on top of his. "I'm thinking about it now."

Brandon's face looked like it might split in half from the width of his own smile. "So, what does this life look like?"

Joan thought for a moment. "Well, I'm the homeowner here, so I guess you should move in with me."

He raised his eyebrows, glancing at her sideways. "Really? Great! I mean, you don't think that's fast?"

"Fast? We've known each other for thirty years!"

"Fair enough," he conceded. "I accept."

"There are two things I want to do once we're for sure curse-free," Joan declared.

"Oh, yeah? Tell me more."

"Three things. There are three things I want to do."

"Well?"

She held up a finger. "Number one – I want to kick all of those whackadoos out of my house."

"Our house," he reminded her.

"Yes. Of course. I want *us* to kick them out of *our* house."

"And then?"

Joan held up a second finger. "And then I want you to move all of your stuff out of your crappy apartment and into our house.

Except for that hideous green chair. You can drop that off at St. Vinnie's on your way over."

"I love that chair," Brandon protested. "My mom gave me that chair."

"She did? I didn't know that." Joan chewed on her bottom lip. "Can we reupholster it?"

"Yeah, okay." He grinned at her. "Look at us – compromising like a couple of pros. What's the third thing?"

"Four things. I have four things, actually."

Brandon laughed. "Okay, what's number three?"

"A martini," said Joan. "I want to relax in a perfect fall evening on my – our – back patio with a perfect martini."

"Mmm. Sounds fantastic. Gin, I assume?"

Joan frowned. "I'm insulted you have to ask. Of course gin. Vodka martinis are a travesty."

"My apologies. And top-shelf, right? Hendrix?"

She shook her head. "Local. I want a local gin, made within fifty miles."

"Shouldn't be a problem. That's why we live in Oregon, right? A boozerie on every corner! I think I've got a couple of local gins in my liquor collection. Dirty?"

"Not quite," said Joan. "Just a hint of olive juice. Not dirty, per se, but slightly sullied."

"Everything worth a damn is slightly sullied," agreed Brandon.

"Exactly. And two olives."

"I think you're right, Joan. That is the perfect martini. You're an adorable genius." Brandon turned the car into Joan's driveway – soon to be their driveway – pulling up behind Veronica's silver SUV, and turned the car off. "What's number four? Are we sticking with four?"

"Yeah. Number four is to live happily ever after."

He unbuckled his seat belt and leaned toward her. Just before his lips touched hers, he whispered, "I'm in."

Chapter 5

As Joan stepped into her house a few minutes later, she frowned at the echoing silence. She usually enjoyed the echoing silence of her home, but she wasn't expecting it this time. Where was everyone?

Joan glanced at Brandon and saw puzzlement mirroring her own. She carefully set down the paper bag of magical supplies on the coffee table, and Brandon set down the stacked totes from Wendy's house beside it.

"It's too quiet," he said. "You don't think...?"

She shook her head. "Mrs. Olsen couldn't have gotten here, could she? She doesn't know where we are, does she? And besides–"

Joan heard the back door open, and she held a finger to her lips, listening. She beckoned Brandon into a corner, grabbing a large book off the shelf beside her and then creeping up next to the doorway leading to the kitchen, waiting for the interloper to reveal themself.

She heard footsteps approach, and raised the book over her head, ready to defend her man, her home, and herself, in that order.

A familiar sneeze sounded, and Sadie walked through the doorway, pulling out her tissues.

"Bless you," said Joan, automatically.

Sadie pivoted toward Joan and raised an eyebrow.

Joan lowered the book, a rueful smile twitching the corners of her mouth. "Oh, hi."

Her best friend snatched the volume out of her hand, studying the cover and then flipping through the pages. "*The Complete Works of William Shakespeare*? Really, Joanie? You were going to bash my head in with the biggest book in the world?"

Joan shrugged. "I thought you might have been Mrs. Olsen."

Finn poked their head around the corner. "Why would you think she was Mrs. Olsen?"

"We just saw her in Salem," said Brandon. "She's in Oregon."

Sadie slammed the tome shut. "What? Are you kidding?" Her voice spiraled upward in volume and octave. "Let me get this straight. You saw Mrs. Olsen in Salem and then drove all the way back to Alexandria, and now you're just calmly standing here telling us about it? Did your phones spontaneously combust? Why the hell didn't you text us? What if she was here?" She shook the book at them with both hands. "Did you think even the bard was going to be able to do anything at all against her?"

The front door opened, and Derek and Veronica entered.

Veronica strode to the coffee table and picked up the sack of magical supplies. "What are you all just standing around for? Wendy's out back, waiting for this stuff."

Sadie spun around. "Mrs. Olsen is in town."

Veronica dropped the bag, spilling plastic baggies full of herbs across the hardwood floor. "Where is she? How do you know? Did she see you?"

"Apparently Joan and Brandon saw her in Salem and didn't see fit to call anyone."

"We were distracted," protested Joan. "I'm sorry."

"You're always distracted," said Derek, folding his arms across his lab coat-clad chest. "Answer the question. Did she see you?"

"No," Brandon responded. "We hid. We learned a few things, though."

He quickly filled in the others on the events in the magic shop.

Sadie pursed her lips. "We need to know more about this Diana person and her Council of Matriarchs."

"She could have been a valuable ally," frowned Derek. "Did you have to flip her off?"

"Yes," said Joan.

"To be fair," said Brandon, "she didn't seem to mind it that much."

Finn cleared their throat. "Why don't we ask Wendy? Doesn't she work at The Broomstick? She seemed to know about the Council earlier."

"She warned you against angering Diana," Derek pointed out.

"Yeah, yeah," said Joan. "Sometimes I just can't help it. Where is Wendy, anyway?"

"I told you, she's out back," said Veronica. "Waiting for these supplies." She knelt and began to gather up the fallen goods. "Actually, I asked Wendy about the Council earlier, while we were getting everything started."

"What did she say?" Joan crouched to help her.

"They don't sound like very nice people," Veronica said, slowly. "They sound like selfish, greedy old women who really dislike anyone who isn't a witch. And getting onto the Council is no picnic. The Matriarchs are the most conniving, most powerful, most ambitious of the witches."

"Great," said Derek. "And we've angered one of them."

Brandon picked up the plastic crates from Wendy's house. "Well, let's just hope we don't have to deal with her again."

Veronica sat back on her heels. "She also said that the Matriarchs might be the only ones besides Mrs. Olsen who would be able to remove our curse."

Joan stood up and extended a hand to Veronica who picked up the refilled bag and stood too.

"Well," said Finn, cheerfully. "You all will just have to be very annoying, so Mrs. Olsen will agree to undo it. And then no one has to ever interact with any conniving, ambitious old hags. Unless my mother comes to town, that is!"

"Yeah," said Veronica. She looked pensive and a little haunted.

Joan wondered just how bad Finn's mom really was.

As the group moved toward the back door, Sadie finagled her way beside Joan, elbowing her in the side as they walked. "So. You and Brandon seem awfully cozy these past few days."

Joan blushed. She tried to murmur out of the side of her mouth, "I'll tell you about it later."

"What?" Sadie leaned closer. "I didn't quite catch that."

"Not with all these people here," Joan muttered again, still trying not to open her mouth.

Sadie grabbed her hand and pulled her off to the side, into the butler's pantry. Joan glanced at the desk shoved in the corner. There really was a forgotten hamster cage there, and it had been shoved aside to reveal an elderly printer. She was astonished it had worked. Didn't the ink in those things dry up after a few years?

Joan was jolted back to the present moment by Sadie's fingers snapping in front of her face.

"Come on, Joanie! Spill it! What's going on with you and Brandon?" Sadie held up a hand before Joan could respond. "And there are three things I do not want to hear you say." She counted them off on her fingers. "I don't want to hear, 'I don't know,' 'we're just friends,' or 'we'll see what happens.' I am tired of hearing those from you, and I will accept no more excuses. I've talked it over with Veronica and Finn, and we've all decided that it's damn well time the two of you sorted your life out."

Joan fought back a smile as Sadie folded her arms and directed a glare in her direction.

"Well?" Sadie demanded.

"We're moving in together," Joan admitted.

Sadie stared at her for a shocked moment and then let out a shrill shriek of delight that went straight through Joan's head.

Joan winced. "Wow. Uncalled for."

Sadie jumped up and down, clapping her hands and then grabbed Joan's hands and spun her around. Joan stumbled into the desk, dislodging a stack of old receipts, and ended up smacking straight into Ed, who was in the process of rushing into the room with a cast-iron pan brandished over his head.

"What's going on?" he demanded. "I'm here!"

"You certainly are," said Sadie. "But why are you here, and why are you threatening us with a frying pan?"

He lowered the pan. "I heard a scream."

"And you thought we were being attacked by a cartoon cat?" Joan raised an eyebrow.

"My hero!" Sadie clasped her hands in mock-adoration and fluttered her eyelashes.

Ed shrugged and hefted the pan. "I think I could do some damage with this bad boy." He glanced around, his eye falling on the hamster cage. "This is a weird room. What are you guys doing in here, anyway?"

"It's supposed to be a pantry, but Joanie doesn't cook," said Sadie.

Beth bustled in, clearly on a mission. "Oh, good, Joan, I found you. I'm wondering if you have any more rugs for the..." She trailed off, looking around the pantry and backing away from a crooked stack of lawn flamingos in the corner. "Where are we? What is this place?"

Finn poked their head around the corner. "There you are. We could use a few more hands in the back woods. Oh, my god. What is this room?"

Joan raised her hands in defeat. "It's a nothing room. We're coming."

Sadie nudged Joan. "We're going to talk more later, never you fear."

As Joan lagged behind the others, following them through the kitchen, she couldn't help but notice when Sadie caught up to Finn and whispered something in their ear.

Finn directed a sunny grin toward Joan and gave her a thumbs up. So much for keeping everyone focused on the task at hand.

Derek was going to be pissed. Oh, well. Derek was a stick in the mud.

Joan returned Finn's smile, perking up a little as they trooped across the back yard. It was about time the old goat shed got some use. Joan had always wanted goats, but somehow just hadn't gotten around to getting any. She kept it clean and in good repair anyway, just in case.

It was a perfect holding cell. It still smelled a little bit like goats from the previous owner, but that just made it more likely Mrs. Olsen would want to get out and would give them what they wanted.

She stepped through the door into the crowded room and raised her eyebrows. The old shed had been completely transformed into a bizarre combination of cozy and creepy. Someone had raided her garage and found all of the furnishings from her childhood bedroom.

There was her white-painted twin bed, complete with its ruffled pink bed skirt,. They had covered it with her threadbare fairy princess sheets and pillowcase. Beside the bed was the matching pink-and-white nightstand. And they had even dragged in the corresponding dresser and bookcase.

Then they had covered the frilly furniture with skulls, jars of eyeballs, and other nightmarish spell components. "Well, my childhood is officially ruined," said Joan.

"Sorry," said Wendy, who was working with Veronica, unpacking more macabre objects to line Joan's bookcase. "It was all we could find."

"Did you have to hang up the pictures too, though?" Joan nodded toward a cartoonish painting of Briar Rose poised to prick her finger on the dread spindle. "I thought we agreed not to torture her."

"You don't like it?" Beth asked. She adjusted the position of a rag rug on the floor. "I thought the walls just looked a little bare. And you have to admit the fairy tale theme fits."

"Excuse me," said Wendy as she bumped into Derek, who was plugging in some kind of machine. "Honestly, is all this really necessary?"

"Yes, it's necessary," he snapped.

"What is?" said Joan. "What are you doing?"

Ed gestured toward the device. "That's one of mine. It measures energetic frequencies in the air. Derek wants to see what happens when the spells take effect."

"We owe it to the scientific community to take advantage of this unique opportunity to observe witchcraft at work," said Derek, setting the toaster-size device on top of the dresser directly between the eyes of the badger.

"Oh, no, you don't," said Wendy. "Those eyeballs need to stay together."

"Well, where can I put it?" Derek asked.

"I can think of somewhere for you to shove it," she said, glaring at him. "This crap is just in my way. And I don't owe science shit."

Derek pulled himself up to his full height, directing a stern stare into Wendy's eyes that would have frozen a wildfire.

Wendy just crossed her arms and raised an eyebrow. "I grew up with a champion glare master. I'd love to see you and my grandpa go head to head in a staring contest someday. In the meantime, you're not going to intimidate me that way. And just for trying, I'm declaring your stupid science banned from this shed."

"You cannot ban science, madam!" Derek gasped.

"Tell that to Kansas," she replied, maintaining eye contact with him as she tossed a handful of herbs into each corner of the room.

"Okay," said Veronica, clapping her hands. "This shed is too crowded. Wendy, who do we really need in here? Everyone else can leave."

"I'm almost set up," Wendy said, consulting her tablet. "I think. I mean, I've never actually done this before."

"Wait, what?" said Beth. "I thought you said you knew how to do it."

"I do. In theory." Wendy shrugged. "I'm following the directions. And most of my spells usually turn out the way they're supposed to."

"Most?" Derek raised an eyebrow.

"This isn't like baking a cake," said Beth. "These are dangerous forces you're playing with!"

"You think I don't know that?" Wendy snapped. "I don't have to do this at all, you know. I'm trying to make things right. And I'm doing the best I can!"

"Hey, hey." Ed stepped between the glowering women. "Let's all just take a deep breath and chill out. Wendy, I'm sure it's all going to be great. Everyone else, Veronica's right – most of us don't need to be here. Let's give the witches some space."

Ed began deftly herding people out of the shed. Before she knew it, Joan found herself out on the lawn, standing beside Sadie and Brandon. Beth and Derek followed, and then Ed leading a reluctant Finn by the hand.

"Veronica might need me," they fretted.

"You know as well as I do what Veronica is capable of," soothed Ed. "She's got that witchy gene, just like Wendy."

"But–"

Just then, Wendy and Veronica rushed out into the yard, Wendy waving her ringing cell phone over her head. "It's her!" she yelled. "Marian is calling me!"

CHAPTER 6

The entire group froze for a moment, the tinkling sound of the ringtone filling the crisp autumn air.

"Are you going to answer it?" asked Joan, finally.

"Should I?" said Wendy. "Are we ready for her?"

"Don't you know that better than us?" said Sadie.

"Yeah, I guess we are ready. Everything's just about set up." Wendy stood, frozen uncertainly, holding her phone at arm's length, staring at it.

It stopped ringing.

"It went to voicemail," said Wendy.

"That's good, really," said Finn. "Now we can find out what she wants and then make a plan based on that."

Joan let out a breath she didn't even realize she'd been holding. Thank goodness for Finn's perpetually clear head. She grabbed for Brandon's hand as they waited.

The seconds ticked by. Wendy continued to hold out her phone away from her body, as though it might come alive and bite her at any moment.

"Does she usually leave a–" Sadie was interrupted by a loud BEEP from the phone.

"There it is!" said Wendy. She clicked frantically through the screens to her voicemail and then hit Play. A tinny voice emerged.

"Put it on speaker," Sadie advised.

Wendy hit another button and Joan jumped as Mrs. Olsen's contralto voice came through clearly.

"–your house. Did you know there's a smashed potted cannabis plant on your front walk? You know that stuff will rot your brain, dear; I wish you wouldn't use it."

"Hypocrite," muttered Joan.

"Brainwashed drone," muttered Ed at the same time.

"I also stopped by the Broomstick," the message continued. "I have to say, dear, I don't think you should work there anymore. I'd forgotten what a harpy that Diana is. I think she may have become a bad influence on you. And it appears that she's a member of the Council now as well, and I don't want you getting on their bad sides. They may be pathetic bickering old women, but they are the most powerful of the bickering old women. Anyway, dear, I have some . . . interesting news and I would prefer to discuss this matter in person, which is why I am in town. Please call me back immediately, so we can get together and confer on this new development."

The recording ended abruptly.

Joan eyed the phone. Even Mrs. Olsen was worried about the Council. Maybe she should have been a little bit nicer to Diana. She replayed their interaction in her head, wondering if it could have gone differently. Probably not. Too late now anyway.

Brandon nudged her, and she snapped back to the present moment to find everyone looking at her.

"Sorry, what?"

"Wendy's going to call her back and tell her to come here," said Brandon. "Do you have any thoughts on what to tell her to get her here?"

Joan shrugged. "Why not tell her the truth?"

"That we're plotting against her and luring her into a trap?" Wendy raised an eyebrow.

"No." Joan shook her head. "Not that you're part of the plot. Just that this is where I live and that there's a group of us who are scheming against her and we're based here. Tell her you've discovered that this is our headquarters. Then claim that we're not here – that you tricked us and sent us to Idaho, since she knows Ed was there at least – and suggest that she join you in laying a trap for us. She'll come out, expecting you to be alone, and then we'll turn the tables."

"That's actually a fantastic idea," said Derek.

"Golly, thanks," retorted Joan. "You don't need to sound so surprised."

"It sounds a little deceptive," objected Beth.

"You do understand what we're doing here, don't you?" said Sadie. "Laying a trap *is* deceptive. She is the bad guy. We're only lying to the bad guy, and not even all that much."

"Well, I don't feel entirely comfortable with it," Beth said, crossing her arms.

"Noted," said Wendy. "Thanks for your input." She hit Call Back on her phone, leaving it on speaker and holding it horizontally in front of her face as it began to ring.

Joan held her breath again, trying not to make any sound. She squeezed Brandon's hand tightly.

"Wendy, dear!" Mrs. Olsen answered the phone. "Thank you for such a swift response. Where are you?"

"I am actually in Alexandria right now," said Wendy. Her voice took on a stiff, businesslike tone to match her mother's.

"Why on Earth would you be in that godessforsaken town?" Mrs. Olsen demanded. "Unless– Do you have a lead?"

"Yes, actually, Marian, I'm–"

"How many times do I have to ask you not to call me that? I am your mother."

"Sorry, yes. Mother. I'm at Joan Sinclair's house. I've discovered that this is where the core group you asked me to focus on has been meeting."

"What are you doing at her home? I hope you're being careful, dear. Are you remembering to use your spells?"

"Yes, Ma- Mother. They're not here. I convinced them that I'd gone away, and they're out of the state, chasing me down."

There was a pause.

"Did you send them to Luzerne, by any chance?"

"Yes! How did you know?"

"I encountered one of them!" Mrs. Olsen's voice filled with triumph. "That's why I rushed out here! I almost had him in my grip, too, but I was so surprised. I really would have appreciated a head's up, dear."

"I'm sorry, Mother," said Wendy, rolling her eyes. "I thought with the festival going on this weekend, it would be a perfect opportunity for a wild goose chase. Anyway, I came here hoping to set a trap for when they return, but I could use your help since you're nearby anyway. Would you come down here and give me a hand?"

"Of course, dear. I'm so proud of you!"

"Thank you, Mother. I'll text you the address."

"Perfect." Mrs. Olsen hung up.

Wendy handed her phone to Joan, who typed in her address and sent it.

"Now we wait," said Wendy.

CHAPTER 7

Thirty minutes later, the plan was in motion. Joan stood very still as she waited for her turn for action.

At this point, Wendy was pacing the driveway, watching for her mother, who would be pulling up at any minute. Once Mrs. Olsen arrived, Wendy would lead her to the shed.

Joan, Brandon, Sadie, and Beth were hiding behind the open doors, and once Wendy and her mother were inside, they would slam the doors shut, bolt them up tightly, and lean against them to keep the pair in.

Wendy would feign confusion to buy some time, while Veronica would dance around outside the shed, performing phase one of the trap – a spell to keep Mrs. Olsen motionless and unable to cast any spells of her own.

Next, Wendy would signal to the trio holding the door shut, and they would open it up. Wendy would exit the shed, set another spell similar to the one she had used to imprison Finn in the bathtub in Idaho around the shed, trapping her inside. Then, Wendy and Veronica would work together to set more spells for dampening magic and reinforcing the invisible cage.

They were taking no chances on Mrs. Olsen's witchcraft.

In the meantime, all of the non-witches in the group would be strengthening their physical security – Finn had rigged up a whole mess of booby traps ringing the shed, which they would activate once Mrs. Olsen was safely inside.

Wendy was sure that her mother would rely heavily on magic and wouldn't consider that others might use more mundane means. If the spells failed, the physical traps would catch her.

Hopefully.

Joan met Brandon's eyes. He gave her a small smile and his arm snaked around her waist, pulling her close. She leaned against his chest, just for a moment.

Then she heard the sound of a car coming up the long driveway. Mrs. Olsen.

Gently, Joan pushed Brandon away and they got into position, ready to slam their side of the doors shut. She could faintly hear Sadie and Beth on the other side, readying themselves as well.

Joan wondered if that was really the best spot for Sadie. Her friend was never very good at standing still. And she needed to stay very, very still for this to work. If Mrs. Olsen suspected for a moment that there was anyone here besides Wendy, they wouldn't be able to catch her off-guard. Wendy was barely trained, Veronica even less so, and none of the others even capable of using witchcraft.

Joan felt her heart beating more quickly as she heard Wendy's contralto voice coming toward them.

"I found something in this shed that I think you're going to find very interesting."

"Oh, really? What have the little twerps been up to?" Mrs. Olsen's voice was filled with scorn, and Joan clenched her fists, fighting the urge to step forward and attack. She focused on the sound of their footsteps on the gravel pathway.

Joan heard a noise from the other side of the doorway. Was that Sadie? Joan mentally pleaded with her friend to just keep still.

"What was that?" said Mrs. Olsen. Her footsteps stopped abruptly.

"I didn't hear anything," said Wendy.

"It must have been the wind," Mrs. Olsen said, but Joan thought she detected a note of doubt in her voice.

Joan squeezed her eyes shut, willing with all her being for this to work.

"Yeah, probably," said Wendy. "Come on, let's go."

Joan heard Wendy's decisive stride move forward, but Mrs. Olsen's slower one didn't follow.

Wendy sighed. "What's wrong, Mother?"

"What's in there?"

There was a pause. Joan bit her lip, hoping Wendy could make up something good. Why hadn't they planned out every scenario? Because they'd thought they would have more time. No one had counted on Mrs. Olsen coming to Oregon right on their heels. The original plan had been to lay the trap and then call her in, so she'd have to drive all the way from Idaho, and they'd have several hours to get everything perfect.

There was so much that could go wrong.

"I found evidence in this shed that one of their group is a witch," said Wendy, finally. "They've been doing spells."

Mrs. Olsen laughed. "Impossible."

"Then it's a pretty big coincidence that there's a shed on this property that has animal skulls and other magical items arranged in mystical configurations. And there are herbs strewn in arcane patterns too. Someone was absolutely using witchcraft in here."

"It can't be." But there was that hint of doubt in Mrs. Olsen's voice again. "None of those students was from a witch family."

"Maybe someone was adopted," suggested Wendy.

Joan smiled slightly. Once again, the small lie based on the overall truth. Mrs. Olsen hadn't counted on Veronica's origins.

"Come in and you'll see what I mean," Wendy repeated.

Another long moment of silence. Joan grabbed Brandon's hand for support, clutching it tightly. He squeezed hers back and they stood together, holding their breath as they waited tensely.

Finally, Mrs. Olsen moved slowly toward the shed.

Joan dropped Brandon's hand and they braced themselves, ready to swing the door shut behind her.

And then, from the other side of the gaping doorway, Sadie sneezed.

"Bless you," Joan called out automatically.

She clamped her hand over her lips, meeting Brandon's wide eyes in a frozen moment.

CHAPTER 8

The next few moments were a whirlwind of action. Mrs. Olsen spun on her heel, yelling, "Who's there? Show yourselves!"

At the same time, Wendy called out, "Veronica, now! We can't wait!"

Joan twisted to face the woods where Veronica was waiting and saw that the untrained witch was already moving forward, clutching Wendy's tablet and chanting the words on the screen as she danced a solo waltz, her voice tense, one arm waving maniacally through the air.

"Let's go," said Brandon, nudging Joan out from their cramped hiding spot behind the barn door. "We need to distract her while Veronica works her spell."

Joan shoved the door out of her way and rushed out into the open. Sadie and Beth were already out there and had each grabbed one of Mrs. Olsen's arms. The older woman was struggling to pull free, and Joan saw with horror the moment in which Mrs. Olsen realized that Wendy had betrayed her.

Mrs. Olsen stopped fighting and narrowed her eyes, staring at her daughter.

Sadie gestured to Beth to take both arms. She pulled off her sweater and used it to tie Mrs. Olsen's hands together. Mrs. Olsen offered no resistance, even as Beth and Sadie each grabbed her by the elbow again.

"You?" she said to Wendy. "Why? And how? I hedged you in with so many spells, you shouldn't have been able to think for yourself for a single moment."

Wendy's face darkened with anger. "I think you just answered your own question, *Mother*. As for 'how,' my new friends helped me."

"Only so that you would help them," said Mrs. Olsen. She glanced over at Veronica. "Young lady, you can stop with the Cinder Hold. I can easily break that."

Veronica glared at her, but continued chanting and dancing, lifting her chin and her voice.

Mrs. Olsen sighed. "Hiberent!" she called out, imperiously.

Veronica froze, mid-dance, her mouth partway open, one foot lifted slightly off the ground. Only her eyes were mobile, darting from side to side.

Joan hoped her lungs and heart worked too.

A rage-filled scream came from across the yard, as Finn barrelled forward from their hiding place near the house.

Mrs. Olsen turned her head toward Finn and rolled her eyes. "Hiberent," she repeated.

Finn halted in place, their mouth still open in a ferocious, now-silenced bellow.

Joan waffled, unsure of the best action. She figured it was best to bide her time until the moment was right, lest she get hibernated or whatever too. She began to ease her way back behind the barn door, slowly so she wouldn't catch Mrs. Olsen's attention.

Brandon followed.

Once they were behind the door, they peered around the edge.

Mrs. Olsen had returned her focus to Wendy. "These people aren't your friends, you know. They only want to use your talents as a witch. They think you can free them from my curse." She turned her head from side to side and lifted her voice to address them all. "She can't help you. Only an experienced witch such as myself can lift a curse of this magnitude. And why should I?"

Beth spoke up from behind Mrs. Olsen. "Because we didn't deserve it. Because we're innocent. Have you no compassion? No empathy?"

"No," said Mrs. Olsen, matter-of-factly, her eyes never leaving Wendy's face. "Those are not qualities I strive for. I had hoped my daughter would inherit my strength of character and my ruthless ambition. Apparently, you've taken after your father instead."

Wendy lifted her chin. "Thankfully, yes."

Mrs. Olsen shrugged. "Well, fortunately, I prepared for this eventuality." She paused, her lips curving upward slightly. "Jackfruit with hollandaise."

Joan frowned. She couldn't have heard that correctly. "What did she say?" she whispered to Brandon.

He shook his head. "It sounded like 'jackfruit with hollandaise.' What kind of nonsense is that?"

Joan shrugged and looked back out around the door. Her eyes widened with horror as she realized that Wendy's face had gone completely slack and her posture rigid.

"It was a trigger code," she breathed. "Wendy's gone full sleeper agent on us."

CHAPTER 9

"Wait a second," Brandon whispered. "Wouldn't she have been a 'sleeper' agent before? Now she's gone all 'awaker' agent. 'Woken' agent?"

Joan turned her head to stare at him. "What?"

"I'm just saying that, as an agent, she is no longer sleeping. She's not a sleeper agent anymore. She's woken up."

"So?"

He dropped his gaze. "So, nothing," he mumbled. "I guess we should probably be focusing on how to save her."

"Damn right! This crazy bitch has pushed her own daughter around long enough! This is the last straw – she's going down!"

"Okay, but weren't we already determined to take her down before?" Brandon pointed out.

"Yes. But now I'm more determined than ever. So just shut up, and let's get down to it!" Joan peaked around the door again to see what she'd missed.

A lot, apparently. Mrs. Olsen and Wendy were getting away, marching down the gravel walkway, just about to round the corner to the driveway. Wendy was hauling a struggling Beth along by the elbow. Beth's hands were now tied up in Sadie's sweater.

Where was Sadie? Joan looked back to the area in front of the shed. Sadie was lying motionless on the ground.

Joan rushed over to kneel beside her best friend, grabbing her wrist and feeling for a pulse. She breathed a sigh of relief when it came through strong. She gently flipped Sadie onto her back, bending over her to listen for breathing.

"Well, she's alive and breathing regularly," Joan said. She turned to Derek as he strode toward her from his own hiding spot. "Did you see what happened? I was distracted."

He frowned. "What could possibly have distracted you in that moment?"

"Do you think a sleeper agent becomes something else once she's woken up?" Joan asked.

Derek paused. "That's an interesting point. Neurologically speaking–"

Ed arrived on the scene. "Who the fuck cares?" he shouted. "Everything has gone fucking pear-shaped, and you're arguing about semantics?"

Sadie sat up suddenly. "What's going on? Why is Ed yelling? Ed doesn't yell."

"You're okay!" said Joan.

"Of course I am. I've been hit harder than that on a Tuesday," Sadie retorted.

"Isn't today Tuesday?" said Brandon.

"Today is Monday," said Derek. He pulled a pen out of his shirt pocket and held it up in front of Sadie's face. "Okay, Sadie, I want you to follow the pen with your eyes for me."

"Oh, fine, I'll do the whole concussion protocol thing, but then we gotta unfreeze Veronica and Finn, rescue Wendy, and get Mrs. Olsen good and kidnapped for realsies." Sadie followed the pen with her eyes as she spoke.

"What is the date today?" asked Derek.

"I have no idea," said Sadie. "But I never know that."

He raised an eyebrow. "The month, at least?"

"September."

"And do you know where you are?"

"Joanie's backyard. Come on, ask me something challenging!" Sadie grinned.

"I thought the date was challenging," said Derek.

"Touchè."

Derek stood up. "Well, I don't think you have a concussion. Your snarkiness remains intact."

Joan reached out a hand and helped Sadie sit up. "You missed one, by the way. We need to rescue Wendy and Beth."

"What happened to Beth?" Sadie looked around the yard.

"She went berserk when Wendy conked you over the head," said Ed. "So Wendy and Mrs. Olsen dragged her away."

"Beth did? That's so sweet!" said Sadie. "I would have thought Joan would be the one to go berserk over me."

"Focus, please," sighed Derek. "We need a plan. The first person we need to rescue is Veronica. We can't do any magic without her, and we'll need magic to undo whatever spell Mrs. Olsen has on Wendy right now."

Joan stood up and walked over to the frozen Veronica, whose eyes followed her the whole way. Well, at least Veronica didn't have a concussion either. "How can we unfreeze her without magic, though?"

Brandon reached out and pried Wendy's tablet from Veronica's rigid fingers. "Maybe there's something on here about a reversal."

"I was under the impression that only someone with witch genes was able to perform these spells," Derek pointed out.

Ed raised his hand. "What about magery?"

Joan spun around. "Yes! Wendy said that anyone could learn magery, as long as you have an aptitude for it."

"Yeah, but we've been looking for this kind of thing for years," objected Brandon. "And we have yet to find any kind of concrete information on how to actually use it."

"Wendy's dad's family are mages, though, right?" said Sadie. "Maybe we could get in touch with them."

Brandon hit an icon on Wendy's tablet, opening up a social media app. "Maybe we could find someone on here who could help us."

Derek cleared his throat. "This is all very hypothetical and sounds time-consuming. Why not contact this Diana person at the magic shop?"

"Because she's a horrible person who hates me?" said Joan. "And everyone seems to think we should steer clear of her and her Council?"

"She's the only witch we know who might help," said Beth.

"She won't help, though," said Brandon. "We already asked her at the shop."

"Maybe under these new circumstances, though," said Ed. "You said she didn't like when witches drew attention to themselves with nonmagical types, right?"

"Because then they'd find out that witches exist," said Joan. "But we all already knew."

"Veronica's a pretty big deal in LA," Sadie pointed out. "If she's up here, frozen, and never comes back, a whole bunch of celebrities are gonna be wondering where their spiritual guru is. That's gonna draw some attention."

"Good point," said Ed. "I think we should call her. Just not Joan."

"Fine," said Brandon. "She didn't seem as pissed off at me. I'll call." He pulled his phone out of his pocket and searched for The Broomstick, clicking on the phone number on their website.

He held the phone up to his ear, his face taking on that blank inwardly focused expression of anyone waiting for someone to answer a call. After a moment, he glanced up. "Voicemail. I'll just leave a message."

He paused, looking around at the small crowd watching him. "It's a really long recording."

He sighed. "No, I don't want to leave a callback number. Does anyone ever leave a callback number? What even is that?"

After another pause, he finally began his own recording. "Hi. Diana, this is Brandon Barber. Wendy's friend? I was in your shop this morning with my girlfriend? The one who flipped you off. Anyway. Um. She's sorry. And we're in a bit of a new pickle, magically speaking. So, if you could give us a call back, and maybe come out to Alexandria, well, it's just outside of town anyway, our only witch here is, um, incapacitated in a magical sort of way, and we don't really know how to fix that, and, um, so, yeah, just call me back. Please. Thanks. Okay. Bye."

"Well, that was completely awkward," laughed Sadie.

"And I am not sorry," said Joan.

"Voicemails are always awkward," Brandon said. "And that was just one of those little white lies you tell when you need a witch who might hate you to come around to your side."

"Well, we're back to square one," said Derek. "At least until she calls us back."

Sadie wandered over to Veronica, peering into her face and giving her a sympathetic half-smile. "Isn't there something we can do to at least make her more comfortable?" She shook Veronica's arm, and it moved a tiny bit. "Hey! Did you see that? Maybe we can change her position, so at least she isn't standing so weird. We could sit her down on the bench over there. And Finn too."

Joan snapped her fingers. "Wait a second! Do you remember in the hotel the other night? When we all went mute in the middle of that reversal spell?"

"What about it?" said Brandon.

"She kept mouthing the words to the spell, even though no sound was coming out, and the spell still worked," said Joan.

"You're saying we could just move her jaw to form the words of a spell?" Derek looked thoughtful. "It didn't seem like a very complicated spell – just one word and no movements. 'Hiberent' is Latin for 'stop.' Maybe if we got Veronica to mouth the word for 'go?'"

"Which is...?" Brandon prompted.

"Let's try 'vado,'" suggested Derek.

"Vado," repeated Sadie. "We're going to have to move her tongue too, to do that *d* sound. This is about to get real weird."

"Just now?" said Joan. "This is just now getting weird to you?"

"The sooner we get Veronica woken up, the sooner we can dispense with this entire situation," Derek pointed out.

"Fair enough. I'm on it." Sadie began sounding out the word, feeling it in her own mouth. "Vado. Vaaaa doooooooooe. Vado. Okay, I'm ready." She squared her shoulders and reached for Veronica's face.

"Is it just me, or do Veronica's eyes look particularly alarmed right now?" Joan murmured to Brandon.

"Do you think she can hear us?" he said.

"If not, all she knows is that we're having a heated discussion right in front of her, and now Sadie's sticking her hand in her mouth," said Ed. "I'd be alarmed too."

Sadie stepped back. "It doesn't seem to have worked."

"There could be a couple of explanations for that," said Derek. He ticked them off on his fingers. "That might not be the counterspell. Maybe she has to know what she's saying and have intention behind it and she can't hear us. It might just take a few minutes to work. Or maybe only Mrs. Olsen can counter this spell since she set it." He sighed, shaking his head. "We simply don't have enough information."

"Well, I'm an optimist," said Ed. "I'm going to go with the first one. Let's try another word. How about 'proficiscor?' Start."

"You know Latin?" said Sadie. "Sexy."

"Why it is sexy that he knows Latin, but not me?" Derek frowned.

"Oh." For once, Sadie seemed at a loss for words. "It totally is. I just, you know, already expected you to know Latin, so I didn't comment on it."

Derek raised an eyebrow. "So you do think I'm sexy?"

"Do you think smoking weed for two days addled his mind?" Brandon muttered to Joan. She choked back a laugh.

"You're just not really my type," said Sadie. "You're very, um."

"Yes?" Derek crossed his arms and narrowed his eyes.

"Serious," Joan supplied. "Sadie's more of a loosy-goosy fun-loving kind of woman, and you're very, very serious, at all times."

Sadie pointed at Joan. "Yes. That. Way too serious."

"I'm sure you're very sexy to other women," put in Brandon. "Beth seemed kind of into you the other day."

"You're quite handsome, in a stern kind of way," said Joan.

Ed cleared his throat. "Hello? How about giving 'proficiscor' a shot?"

"God, yes. Let's do that." Sadie sounded it out. "Pro-fic-i-scor. It's a little more complicated, but I think I can get her to say it. Pro. Fic. I. Scor. Proficiscor." She nodded. "Okay, I've got it."

Joan held her breath as Sadie moved Veronica's jaw, lips, and tongue again and then stepped back.

Veronica collapsed into a heap at Sadie's feet.

Chapter 10

"Princess!" Finn came careening across the yard, skidding to a halt and buckling to their knees beside Veronica's supine figure. They pushed her onto her back and checked for a pulse.

"You're alive," Finn sighed with relief.

Veronica's eyes fluttered open. "Finn?"

"I'm here, princess."

Veronica bolted up into a seated position. "We have to help Wendy and Beth!"

"How much were you guys aware of during that whole thing?" asked Ed.

"I could see and hear," said Finn. "I couldn't move my head, so I only saw what was in my field of vision, but I heard Mrs. Olsen say something that sounded like a vegan brunch order, and then Beth was yelling something, and a minute later Wendy and Mrs. Olsen dragged Beth away."

"The brunch order was a trigger code," said Veronica, grimly. "Wendy was afraid that might have been set up."

"She knew? And she didn't tell anyone?" Joan frowned.

"Doesn't hollandaise have eggs in it?" said Brandon.

"Oh, you can make anything vegan." Veronica perked up. "Our favorite diner, right around the corner from our apartment, does a phenomenal vegan hollandaise with tofu and lemon juice."

"It is not phenomenal," murmured Finn. "Unless you've been vegan for fifteen years and forgotten what the real thing tastes like."

"Well." Veronica pinned her partner in the sunniest glare Joan had ever seen. "It's much healthier."

"Of course, princess," Finn soothed.

"Anyway," continued Veronica, standing up with Finn's help. "We found a spell for the whole sleeper agent thing in the grimoire, but Wendy noticed that Mrs. Olsen hadn't put it in the file she transferred to the tablet. She also neglected to give her the reversal."

"Well, that's suspicious," said Sadie.

"Exactly. We do have the grimoire, however, which includes the reversal, and Wendy connected her phone to the tablet, just in case of exactly this situation, so we can track her phone, find them and reverse the spell. Then Wendy will be the ultimate double agent."

"I can be fun," said Derek, abruptly.

Six heads swiveled, twelve pairs of eyes staring at him.

"What?" said Finn.

"I can be fun," he repeated. "I'm not serious all the time. I have hobbies. I enjoy reading mystery novels and watching old films, some of which are even comedies."

"Look, I'm sorry," Sadie began. "I'm sure you're a hoot and a half. I'm just not interested in–"

Derek waved his hands impatiently. "No, no, I'm not interested in you either. I just– I don't want to be pigeonholed as this uptight, no-fun fuddy-duddy."

Brandon spoke up. "You know, Derek, this feels an awful lot like shenanigans. Focusing on personal stuff when we really should be trying to rescue Wendy and Beth."

"You're right, of course," said Derek, deflating slightly. "I'm sorry."

"No," Brandon protested. "That wasn't a criticism!"

"Welcome to the club." Joan grinned.

Sadie held out a hand toward Derek. He tentatively grasped it, and she shook his hand vigorously. "Well done, sir!"

Derek smiled broadly. "I did a shenanigan!"

"Now, let's get back to business," said Finn.

Brandon handed the tablet back to Veronica. "How do we track her?"

Veronica opened an app and studied the map that popped up. "It looks like they're actually really close by. Just down the road."

"Really? Let me see that," Joan grabbed the tablet. "Oh, that's the old Sigaro farm. It's been for sale for months and has No Trespassing signs all over. I wonder if we could just call in the cops, have her arrested for trespassing, swoop in and grab our friends and be done with it."

"And if Mrs. Olsen just freezes the cops like she did me and Finn?" Veronica shook her head. "No, there's too much that can go wrong. Have you been there before, Joan?"

"Yeah, they used to have bonfires every summer. Me and Brandon went to a couple of them."

"Brandon and I," muttered Derek.

"Dude," said Ed. "You're undoing all your good work."

"Hey, wait a second." Finn held up a hand. They stood for a moment, their hands moving through a complicated progression of gestures, their eyes blinking rapidly.

"What's–" Derek began.

"Shhh!" Veronica waved him into silence. "They're processing an idea," she whispered. "Finn's brilliant, you know."

Finn held out their hand for the tablet. "I think I know how to incapacitate Mrs. Olsen with only one spell, instead of this complicated cocktail of witchcraft. Let me see that for a moment, princess."

Veronica handed it over, and Finn opened up the grimoire document, flipping through the pages at a furious pace, Veronica leaning close to see over their shoulder. Finally, they stopped. "There! What do you think?"

Veronica whistled. "That could work. I think we have all this stuff in the shed. Except for– No, we can use the badger!"

"If we can pull this off, it'll be much more effective, right?" said Finn.

"Absolutely."

Joan craned her head, trying to catch a glimpse of the tablet. "What'll be more effective?"

Veronica lifted her head, a huge grin spreading across her face. "How big is that hamster cage of yours?"

CHAPTER 11

An hour later, Joan climbed over the fence that divided her land from the Sigaros'. Veronica handed over two plastic totes from the other side and then climbed after her. Joan picked hers back up again with a groan and began to trudge through knee-high grass toward a distant barn. She was covered in dust and bits of bracken.

"They're never going to sell this place if they can't be bothered to come out here with a mower," she remarked.

"I think it has a lovely, rustic charm," said Veronica, who hadn't even broken a sweat. The grass seemed to be parting in front of her. "Why did they move?"

"Pete's back started giving him issues, and they couldn't keep up the farm. They moved in with their daughter in town. She was a couple of years ahead of us in school. Mindy Sigaro. Remember her?"

"Yeah, we did cheer together. Kind of a snooty bitch. I mean, I was too at the time, because high school, but she blew me out of the water."

"She's still pretty snooty," said Joan. "Even though she really peaked in high school and no longer has anything to be snooty about."

Veronica shrugged. "She's probably just really unhappy with her life and feels like she has to pretend she isn't."

Joan thought this through. "I feel like she'd be happier if she wasn't snooty and people liked her."

"People are idiots, sweetie," said Veronica. "I think this is close enough."

Joan carefully set down her tote on a tree stump. As she straightened, she squinted at the barn, which was now about a hundred yards away. She couldn't see any signs of habitation, but that's where the tracker had led them.

Just then, the door opened, and Wendy emerged, her face still blank, her motions somewhat robotic.

"Duck," Joan hissed, throwing herself onto the ground and peering up through the tall grass.

Veronica hit the deck beside her. "If I get bugs crawling in my clothes, I'm going to lose it," she warned.

"Oh, grow some ovaries." Joan rolled her eyes. "Bugs aren't going to hurt you."

"What if they bite me?"

"Then you'll have an itchy bump for a couple of days and then it'll go away."

"I could get malaria," she pointed out.

"Well, then I guess you'll die," said Joan, heartlessly. "You're being ridiculous. Do you see Wendy out there? She's literally been taken over by her mother. And you're worried about some teeny little insects?"

"Right. Okay. Your tote has the stuff for the first spell. Let's get it set up." Veronica inched her way over to the stump and pulled the crate down onto the ground to rummage through it. She pulled out a couple of jars of herbs and some bits of animals, checking the ancient book a couple of times as she arranged everything in a semi-circle in front of them.

"Lucky that one's in English," remarked Joan.

"Yeah, the tablet has all of them translated, but since this one wasn't in there, we could have had some real issues. Did you know Wendy has had to learn four languages in the last two years?" Veronica cocked her head as she examined a skull. "Do you think this one is the badger or the horse?"

"Look at the teeth," said Joan. "That's the right one."

"I guess if I want to be a witch, I'm going to have to learn that stuff too," said Veronica.

"Are you going to be a witch?" asked Joan, surprised. "After all of this?"

"I haven't decided. I mean, I have the ability, right? So it seems like if you can be a witch, why wouldn't you? It's a pretty cool thing to be. I talked to Wendy about it. She thinks the older witches will be fighting over who gets to train me. It would be a big life change, though. Finn and I would have to move up here. And I would want to learn from the best, which would be these Matriarchs, right? But they sound awful."

"What does Finn think about that?" Joan cocked her head.

Veronica scooted back a little and examined the arrangement of herbs, skulls, and birds' wings, then compared it to the diagram in the book. She answered quickly. "I haven't talked to them about it yet. Okay, I think this is right. I'll have to stand up to do the dance, though."

"Veronica! You have to discuss this with your partner!"

"Oh, look whose talking," Veronica scoffed. "You and Brandon have been dancing around for years with no communication whatsoever, and you're going to come in and tell me how to–"

Joan shook her head. "Don't deflect this back on me. You know I'm right."

Veronica sighed. "I know. They're going to hate it, though, I just know it. Let's deal with one crisis first, and then I'll deal with the next. Convincing my partner, whose mother is a conniving bitch who made their life hell for years, that we should move to a new state and hang out with a bunch of new conniving bitches for the next several years."

"You're right. One thing at a time." Joan looked back toward the barn. "Wendy's still out here. It looks like she's–" She squinted. "Gathering plants. Great, probably for some new and exciting spell for Mrs. Olsen to try out on us."

Veronica looked up. "I guess we'd better stop her, then. Listen, we don't know if Wendy has orders to watch out for us. If she does, she'll react when we stand up – either leaving to alert her mom or attacking us, depending on what her instructions are. If not, she'll just ignore us. She can't act without explicit instructions in this state."

"Okay." Joan nodded. "If she attacks, I'll draw her away from you so you can finish the spell. If she starts heading inside to tell Mrs. Olsen, I'll tackle her."

"Great." Veronica rolled onto her side to face Joan, reaching out to grasp both of her hands. "Sweetie, can I just say that it has been an honor working with you these past few days? I never really liked you much before, but I guess I never bothered to get to know you. I thought you were a bit of a negative Nancy, but it turns out you're a badass."

"Yeah, you too," said Joan, gently squeezing Veronica's hands in return. "On all counts. Except for the negative Nancy thing. I thought you were an overly positive Polyanna. And I never knew a vegan could even be a badass."

Veronica smiled. "Shall we?"

"Let's do this shit."

Joan dropped Veronica's hands and tried to spring gracefully to her feet as Veronica was doing. Instead, her right knee buckled slightly, and she lurched sideways, stumbling forward several feet before regaining her balance. She looked up to see if Wendy had noticed.

Wendy had dropped the basket she had been carrying and was staring at her.

"Hey, friend," said Joan. "What's up?"

Wendy took a step toward her, stretching her arms out like a zombie.

Joan stepped back. She could hear Veronica chanting behind her, beginning the spell to release Wendy from her thrall.

As Joan moved back again, Wendy kept pace with her. Veronica's voice was closer now, so Joan stepped to the side, rather than run into whatever dance the budding witch was performing at the moment.

Apparently, Wendy wasn't as into that. Her face twisted into a bizarre scowl, her eyes scrunched up, her lips drawing back into a silent snarl.

Joan froze, eyes wide, her heart speeding up, and waited to see what Wendy would do next. She watched as Wendy's expression continued to contort from one grotesque grimace to another, her pose still reminiscent of a cheesy horror movie. Finally, her visage landed in an intense narrow-eyed glare, and Wendy lowered her head and her arms and charged straight for Joan.

CHAPTER 12

J oan yelped and jumped one pace to her left.

Wendy's course didn't change, and she charged right past Joan. She stumbled and whirled around, breathing heavily. Her gaze fixed on Joan again and she squared her shoulders, lowered her head again like a bull, and hurtled toward her.

This time, Joan was ready for her and dodged easily.

Wendy spun around again, her nostrils flaring, chest heaving as she stared at Joan.

Joan gave her a little smile in return and held out a hand, blinking slowly at Wendy, like she was a frightened cat. "Hey, Wendy. It's okay. You know me, right? It's me, Joan. I'm not going to hurt you. We're trying to get this spell lifted. You just gotta give Veronica another minute, okay?"

Shaking her head slowly, Wendy growled.

Joan lowered her hand. "You're going to run at me again, aren't you?"

Wendy lurched forward, flailing her arms toward Joan. Joan quickly stepped aside, and Wendy stumbled past her again. Joan grabbed Wendy's arm to stop her from falling, and in that instant, Wendy's body went rigid.

The pair of them crashed to the ground, Wendy pinning Joan down. Joan stared up at her friend's face, searching for signs of awareness.

Wendy blinked. "Joan?" she said, groggily.

"Wendy? Are you in there?"

"Yes!" Wendy jumped to her feet and extended her hand to Joan, who grasped it gratefully, pulling herself up as well. "I'm here! Sorry I attacked you."

"No worries. You weren't yourself," said Joan, brushing herself off.

"I know. I tried to stop. I couldn't."

Veronica ambled over to them. "Welcome back, Wendy."

"Welcome yourself!" Wendy gave Veronica a brief hug. "You did great. Do you guys have a plan moving forward?"

"We sure do," said Veronica, her smile widening.

Joan and Veronica outlined their plan to Wendy.

"That's crazy," said Wendy. "It would stop her from doing any spells – including reversing your curse. But I must admit it has a certain amount of panache."

"I figure we can teach her sign language so when she's ready to cooperate she can let us know," said Joan.

"What's to stop her from just saying she'll reverse it and then not doing it?" asked Wendy. "I gotta say, the way she's been talking about you." She bit her lip. "I feel a lot less confident now that we'll be able to convince her at all. If you go this route, you might piss her off so much that she'll never cave."

"Well, it'll at least buy us some time," said Joan. "Maybe once she's out of the way, you and Veronica will be able to reverse it yourselves."

Wendy shook her head. "Veronica's got real power and I'm no slouch either, but a curse reversal takes a lot more power and discipline than the actual curse, especially if you're not the one who set it to begin with. I don't think we'd be able to figure it out in time. You'll need an experienced witch at the top of her game."

"Like someone on the Council?" said Veronica.

"Yeah," Wendy snorted. "Good luck with that."

Joan crossed her arms. "Look, this is the plan we've made. Do you have a better idea?"

Wendy shook her head. "I guess not. At least this is pretty quick. It'll work better than our original plan would now that she's on her guard. Let's get moving, then."

"Good luck, you guys," said Veronica. "I'll see you in maybe half an hour or so."

"Yeah, good luck to you too," said Joan. She turned to Wendy. "Try not to rough me up too much, okay?"

"I don't think I need to rough you up at all," said Wendy. "Marian's got Beth in a horse stall, in a simple box spell like I used on Finn in Idaho. She had me set the spell, so I can take it down and put you in with her. Marian will assume that I've put it back up, but you guys will be able to get out once we get Veronica's signal."

"Mrs. Olsen isn't in there?" asked Joan. "Where is she?"

Wendy shrugged. "I have no idea. I guess she didn't feel like she needed to talk to me once I was under her sleeper agent spell."

"You think it's still called that once triggered? We've been arguing about that." Joan followed Wendy toward the barn.

"Huh." Wendy cocked her head, pausing as she opened the door. A waft of musty air drifted out. "I don't know. It doesn't seem that important, once it's actually happened to you."

"Fair enough," said Joan, wrinkling her nose at the smell. "Did a skunk keel over and die in here?"

"I know. Sorry." Wendy led Joan down the length of the barn to the very last stall.

Inside, Beth sat on the floor, leaning against the back wall, her knee-length black dress draped primly over her crossed legs. She looked up as they approached and she studied Wendy carefully. A small smile stretched her lips as she stood up. "Welcome back to your brain, Wendy. Hi, Joan. Nice of you to join us."

Joan cocked her head. "How come I can hear her? We couldn't talk to Finn when they were trapped by the box."

"Really?" Wendy gestured, presumably dissolving the invisible box surrounding the stall. "I must have messed up the spell. Hi, Beth. Sorry I locked you up in here. I hope you don't mind sticking around a while longer."

"That's okay. I'm just glad to see you're feeling more yourself now," she said.

Wendy opened the stall door, holding it open for Joan to enter. "Thanks."

"I take it there's a new plan?" said Beth.

"I'd better get back outside, actually," said Wendy, closing the stall gate back up again. "I need to still be gathering those herbs whenever Marian returns. Joan will fill you in."

Wendy sauntered out the door, and Joan turned to face Beth. It felt awkward to be alone in close quarters with her. They'd never exactly been friends.

Beth gave her a tight smile and sat down again. "So, what's the plan?"

Joan lowered herself gingerly to the floor beside her and quickly filled her in.

"A badger?" Beth stared at her. "Seriously?"

"We figured we didn't have time to go back out and find another skull," said Joan, shrugging. "We had a badger skull, a horse, and an eagle."

Beth pursed her lips, furrowing her brow. "What kind of badger skull is it?"

"What kind? What do you mean?"

"There's the American badger, the European badger, the ferret badger, honey badger…. Some people would mention the stink badger too, but that's actually technically a member of the skunk family." Beth leaned back against the wall. "I didn't finish college, but the two years I was there I majored in zoology with an emphasis on small woodland predators."

Joan eyed Beth with new respect. "I didn't know that."

"Well. Now you do. What kind of badger is it?"

Sighing, Joan ran a hand over her honey-blonde hair, untangling it and dislodging some grass. "Honestly, the only reason we know it's a badger at all is that it's labeled. It didn't give us a genus."

"Species, you mean," said Beth, absently.

"Right. Sorry, I never paid much attention to biology," said Joan. "Too squishy."

Beth smiled warmly, her bright blue eyes crinkling a little at their edges. "You're not supposed to squish the animals, Joan. You're supposed to study them. Anyway, I guess we'll find out what kind of badger it is soon enough."

"Did Mrs. Olsen tell you where she was going or when she'd be back?" Joan asked.

"No, that'd be too easy," said Beth. "She's not a very friendly person, is she? Do you remember what she was like as a teacher?"

"Well, yeah. She was awful. She put a curse on us, remember?" Joan raised an eyebrow. "So, not really my favorite teacher of all time."

"We had her for six months before she cursed us. Did you like her before that?"

Joan shook her head. "Honestly? No. I thought she was a huge bitch."

Beth winced. "Is that necessary? After all, I can't imagine that even you used that word when you were six years old."

"What is that supposed to mean – 'even you?'" Joan crossed her arms, her eyes narrowing.

"Sorry," Beth muttered. "You have to admit you have a pretty terrible potty mouth."

"The only thing I will admit is that I use the best word for the job in any given moment," Joan retorted. "Mrs. Olsen was a bitch. You know it. I know it. Hell, she probably knows it herself. Are you going to sit here and say that she isn't? Let's just put the whole curse situation aside. What word would you use to describe the woman who told Sadie – who was five years old at the time – that she wasn't going to amount to anything because she couldn't spell the word 'cousin?'"

"Wow. She said that to her?" Beth leaned forward. "That's crazy."

"Yup. And I'm just easing you in. Brandon and I were in the high reading group. It was the two of us, Derek, and that girl Sandrine who ended up skipping fourth grade. Every time we met, she would single out one of us, whoever was stumbling a little over the words or whose homework was written out a little less legibly than the others, and tell us that if we didn't improve by the next time, we'd get sent to sit with, and I quote, 'the stupid kids' in the other reading groups. Me and Brandon took turns purposely fucking up so that neither of us would get yelled at two days in a row."

"Gosh!" breathed Beth.

"Really?" said Joan. "'Gosh' is really the word you chose to use there? What about this one? What's the best word to describe this situation? Mindy Sigaro, whose barn we're sitting in right now, had her two years before us, right? She once told me that Mrs. Olsen made all the left-handed kids in her class use their right hands, and then made fun of their handwriting. Apparently, the principal found out and made her stop."

"That is awful," said Beth.

"No, it isn't!" said Joan, rolling her eyes. "It's 'fucked up.' Eggplant is 'awful.'"

"I like eggplant. Anyway, I don't see why you have to be so judgy all the time," said Beth.

That stopped Joan in her tracks. "I'm judgy? You're the judgiest person I've ever met!"

"I am not!" Beth protested. "You are constantly judging me – you think I'm prissy and weak just because I'm Christian!"

"No, I think you're prissy and weak because you dress like an old lady and you say 'gosh' instead of 'holy shit' and you never stand up for yourself," Joan retorted.

"See? You're judging the way I dress! And just because I don't get defensive at every little thing anyone says doesn't make me weak. I just believe in giving people the benefit of the doubt. I don't think everyone is out to get me – maybe they're just having a bad day and lashing out." Beth tossed her head. "I believe in turning the other cheek. But I stand up for other people all the time."

"So do I," said Joan.

"I didn't say you didn't. I'm just saying that I don't prioritize taking offense at everything."

Joan opened her mouth to rebut, then snapped it shut as a rich chuckle filled the air.

Mrs. Olsen had returned.

Chapter 13

"Bravo, my dear daughter," said Mrs. Olsen, glancing toward Wendy, who stood stiffly beside her. "You've captured another one. And they're at each other's throats, like the bickering brats they've been all their lives."

Wendy remained motionless, staring off into space.

Mrs. Olsen sighed. "I must say, I enjoy having an obedient daughter, but I wish I could have left your intelligence intact. Maybe I can tinker with the spell a little bit. Would you like to have some of your mind back, Wendy?"

"Yes, mother," Wendy responded, her face blank, her voice empty of all inflection.

Joan felt a pang of unease. Was Wendy that good of an actor? Or had Mrs. Olsen figured out their ruse and turned her back into an automaton?

Mrs. Olsen smiled at Wendy and reached out to ruffle her hair.

Joan relaxed slightly as she noticed Wendy's minute wince at this transgression against her habitually immaculate appearance. She quickly jumped to her feet to distract Mrs. Olsen before she noticed her daughter's reaction too. "What are you going to do with us?" she demanded.

"I don't need to do anything," said Mrs. Olsen. "All I have to do is keep you here until March. And then you'll be powerless – mute and blind, as my curse resettles on you, for good this time."

"But why?" asked Beth. "Why couldn't you just leave us alone?"

Mrs. Olsen's face twisted. "You never left me alone. All these years, you've been searching for me, chasing me down–"

"The only reason we were looking for you is to ask you to undo the curse!" said Joan. "If you hadn't cursed us in the first place, we wouldn't give a fuck about you!"

"Tsk, tsk, tsk." Mrs. Olsen shook her head. "Such language."

"I know, right?" said Beth.

"Don't agree with her!" Joan put her hands on her hips and glared down at Beth.

"Sorry," Beth muttered. She pulled her knees up, struggling to leverage herself to her feet without allowing her dress to creep up.

Joan sighed and extended her hand.

Beth grasped it and stood. She stepped forward to stand beside Joan and they faced Mrs. Olsen together.

"You are a mean-spirited old biddy who should never have been allowed to work with children," said Beth.

"And you're a terrible mother," added Joan. "No parent worth a damn puts coercion spells on their daughter."

"If Wendy had been willing to work with me, she would have control of her faculties right now," snapped Mrs. Olsen. "It's hardly my fault her mage father didn't instill the proper grit of a true witch in her. I got at her too late."

"Good parents don't get 'at' their children at all," said Beth.

"I don't have to stand here and take this," hissed Mrs. Olsen. "You know nothing about me or the struggles I've faced. You know nothing of witches at all."

"And I thank God for that every day," said Beth.

Mrs. Olsen spun on her heel and strode out of the barn, calling over her shoulder as she walked. "Wendy. Come with me."

Wendy gave Beth and Joan a small grateful smile and then lurched robotically after her mother.

Joan let out a shaky breath. "That woman is terrifying."

"I couldn't tell you were scared," said Beth. "You were great."

"I have a gift for pissing people off," said Joan. "I don't usually do it on purpose. You were really good too."

"Look, I'm sorry about before." Beth bit her lip and cast her eyes toward the ground. "I do actually respect you a lot. You're smart and strong and maybe you're a little bit right about me not sticking up for myself. Sometimes I wish I had your confidence."

"Well, sometimes I wish I had your self-control." Joan smiled ruefully. "I just blurt out whatever pops into my head."

"You have good things in your head," said Beth. "And it's good that we have so many different kinds of people on God's earth."

"See? What is that? We're having a perfectly pleasant conversation, getting to know each other better, finding mutual respect, and then BAM! You gotta bring religion into it? Why?" Joan leaned against the back wall, cocking her head and frowning at Beth.

Beth shrugged. "You want to get to know me better? My religion is part of me. You want to find respect for me? You're going to have to respect that. And I'll meet you halfway. I'll do my best to respect that a lack of faith is part of you."

"I don't have a lack of faith," said Joan. "I have a lack of religion. I have faith in plenty."

"There's no difference to me," Beth said. "I–"

The door opened, and Joan pushed herself away from the wall, leaning sideways to see who was coming in. Brandon and Sadie stumbled into the barn as though shoved from behind.

Joan grinned. So far, so good. They had released Wendy, riled up Mrs. Olsen, and all the players were in place.

Now all they had to do was keep Mrs. Olsen riled up – hopefully keeping her in that sweet spot of angry-enough-to-not-be-thinking-clearly but not angry-enough-to-place-more-curses – and wait for Veronica and Wendy to do their part.

Joan tried not to dwell on specifics of how this could all go wrong as Wendy and Mrs. Olsen followed Brandon and Sadie inside. Instead, she focused on schooling her face into a dismayed expression. "No!" she cried, cringing inside at her overly dramatic tone.

Mrs. Olsen remained in the doorway, a particularly smug angle to her cocked hip and crossed arms. "I'm afraid your plans are all going straight down the toilet, dear."

"Oh, yeah?" said Beth. "Well, you can go straight down a toilet too, for all we care!"

Joan raised an eyebrow. As insults went it was a little derivative. Oh, well, Sadie was here now. Sadie was just as good as Joan at being obnoxious. Possibly even more so.

Wendy opened the stall and shoved Sadie and Brandon inside, making an arcane gesture as she did so, presumably to fool her mother into thinking she was dismantling the invisible box. Joan gave Wendy an encouraging smile as she caught Brandon by the arm before he staggered straight back into the wall.

Sadie did not disappoint. She found her footing right away, pivoted to face Mrs. Olsen, and screamed, "You horrible fucking harpy! You'll pay for this, you pathetic excuse for a human being! We're going to get out of here, and we're going to come after you with everything we have!"

Mrs. Olsen stepped into the barn, her brown eyes narrowing. "You have nothing. You are powerless against me."

"Then why don't you just let us go?" said Brandon. "Leave us alone. We can't hurt you. You're a witch. We're just regular people."

"Because you don't deserve it," said Mrs. Olsen. "And because even a blundering idiot can sometimes do as much damage by accident as a witch could do on purpose."

"Well, you better watch your back," said Sadie, dancing forward.

Joan grabbed her arm to stop her from leaning over the stall gate and showing that the invisible box wasn't there anymore.

"Yeah," said Beth.

Sadie ignored her. "Because we have a powerful witch coming."

"You don't know any witches," dismissed Mrs. Olsen, turning away.

"Yes, we do!" said Brandon. "Does the name Diana Peregrine mean anything to you?"

Mrs. Olsen spun around, striding toward them. "You miserable little brats. You called in the Council of Matriarchs? You are playing with forces you cannot possibly understand."

"Cliché much?" muttered Joan.

Sadie grinned. She adopted a boxer's stance, putting up her fists and bouncing from foot to foot. "That's right, bitch. And those forces are headed straight for you." The effect of the threat was ruined slightly as she sneezed immediately afterward.

Joan stopped herself from her habitual response. It had ended badly last time.

Mrs. Olsen stared at them, breathing heavily. "You did call her. You idiots! I'll have to–" She stopped abruptly, turning around and rushing out the door, leaving Wendy standing in the middle of the room.

As the door slammed behind her, Wendy gave her erstwhile prisoners a sunny grin. "That was amazing! Did you really get Diana on your side?"

Brandon shook his head, tossing an arm around Joan's shoulders. "Unfortunately, no. She did call me back, but I think I made things worse. She seemed a little bit annoyed."

Wendy frowned. "That's not good. Diana is dangerous. She just might decide you're a threat that needs to be neutralized. I wish you'd talked to me before calling her."

"You weren't exactly available for questioning," pointed out Sadie. "Not that I'm blaming you for that."

"Let's just hope she decides to leave it alone," said Wendy. "At this point, I think that's our best-case scenario here."

"No chance she'd decide to help us out?" asked Beth.

Wendy shook her head. "I mean, she does really hate Marian. But her disdain for ordinary people will trump that every time."

"And there's no chance she'd stick her neck out for you?" asked Brandon. "She's your boss, after all, and you are a witch."

"A witch who can't handle her own mother is not a witch worth helping," said Wendy. "Above all, the Council respects the strong. Plus her daughter is my age – if I'm out of the way, that's one less rival for Carrie."

"What a terrible way to live," said Beth.

Wendy shrugged. "That's witches. Honestly, the more time I spend with my mother's people, the less I blame my dad for keeping me away from her."

Sadie reached over the stall door to give Wendy's shoulder a sympathetic squeeze and Joan gave her a little half-smile of empathy.

Wendy returned the smile for an instant and then briskly returned to business. "Well, so we're on our own. What else is new?"

Joan sighed. "At least we're used to that. How is everything else going? Wait, I thought Derek and Sadie were supposed to be the next people captured. What are you doing here?" She frowned at Brandon.

"What's wrong, babe? You're not happy to see me?" He laughed.

"I am! It's just that Derek's so much better at being irritating."

Sadie shrugged. "As it turns out, Derek's also good at following diagrams to a T, so Veronica decided she wanted him to help set up the spell."

"I guess that's unsurprising," said Joan. "Is it a really complicated spell?"

"Very," said Brandon.

"So lots of things could go wrong?" said Beth.

"Oh, yes," affirmed Sadie. "Absolutely."

"Sounds about right," said Joan. She turned to Wendy. "Speaking of which, I guess you're stuck in here with us. You can't go back out there without Mrs. Olsen giving you orders, can you?"

"Crap. You're right." Wendy bit her lip. "So I won't be able to help sneak them in. And I'll be in here whenever she comes back, which means she might give me orders and I'll have to pretend to follow them."

Joan shook her head. "We'll just have to make sure our diversion is so fantastic that she forgets all about you and comes after us single-mindedly."

"Any ideas?" asked Sadie.

"We could pretend to be on the phone with Diana when she comes in," suggested Beth. "That would really cream her corn."

"Or we could be at each other's throats," said Joan. "A good old fashioned brawl is always distracting."

"Better yet," Brandon put in, "you and I could be making out hardcore. You know what they say – sex always sells."

Sadie wiggled her eyebrows at Beth. "Guess that would leave you and me. What do you say?"

Beth rolled her eyes. "Pass. No offense."

"Wait a second," said Wendy. "Go back. What did you say before, Joan?"

"A brawl?"

"Throats...." Wendy snapped her fingers. "I think I know what I did wrong before – why sound didn't travel through the barrier when I trapped Finn in the box in Idaho!"

"Oh, hey, I brought your tablet along," said Sadie. "We transferred all the spells over to Veronica's phone so she has them, and I figured you might want it." She dug around in her gigantic green leather purse, pulling out the tablet.

Wendy grabbed it from her and opened up her spell file, flipping through a few pages before she found the one she wanted. She studied it intently. "Yeah. Yeah, I think I can do this again." She examined a grouping of arcane items and herbs spread across the floor off the to side and made a couple of adjustments to the configuration. Then she looked up, grinning. "You guys do your distraction. As soon as Derek and Veronica get in here, I'll put up a barrier so Marian can't hear what they're doing and won't be able to stop them."

The barn door opened. Wendy hurriedly threw the tablet aside, a panicked look flashing over her face before it became carefully blank and she resumed her neutral robot posture.

CHAPTER 14

Joan also panicked – they hadn't settled on an actual plan for the diversion. She chose one of the options at random, reaching up to grab Brandon's head and pulling it down to mash her lips against his. Panic-kissing, as it turns out, wasn't as pleasant as regular kissing.

Behind her, she could hear Beth and Sadie arguing loudly. Apparently, they'd gone with her brawl plan.

"Well, you're ugly and dumb, and I hate you," yelled Beth. Not super original, but in the moment, it wasn't bad.

"You're a little stick-in-the-mud," retorted Sadie. "Who ruins everything." A little on the nose.

Brandon wrapped his arms around Joan's waist and softened the kiss, and suddenly she was too distracted to pay attention to the fake fight going on behind her. She closed her eyes and focused solely on the warmth of Brandon's lips, which tasted like coffee and Brandon, two of her favorite things.

Her hands moved from the back of his head down to his neck and then to his strong shoulders, her fingers trailing past the short sleeve of his black t-shirt and down his tattooed arm.

And then she was jolted out of the kiss as Sadie crashed into her and the three of them went tumbling into a tangled heap on the dirty floor.

Joan lifted her head, gingerly touching her bottom lip, which either she or Brandon had bitten in the fall. Her finger came away red and she tasted iron.

"What the hell is going on in here?" demanded Mrs. Olsen from the other side of the gate.

"We don't have to answer to you," shrilled Beth. She had also been knocked to the floor by the wave of power that had burst through the stall, and she sat up, holding the back of her head.

Joan struggled to her feet, pushing herself up on what turned out to be the top of Sadie's head.

"Ow," said Sadie.

"Sorry." Joan reached down and helped Sadie and Brandon to their feet, then stepped over and helped Beth up too.

Sadie strode to the front of the horse stall and glared at Mrs. Olsen, her shoulders square, hands on her hips. "She's right. It's none of your damn business."

"She's right? You were just screaming obscenities at her."

"I wouldn't call them 'obscenities,'" Sadie objected.

"I would," Beth muttered.

"Anything you can say on regular TV isn't really an obscenity," said Joan.

"You can't say that on regular TV, can you?" said Mrs. Olsen.

"Damn, Sadie, what were you calling her?" demanded Joan.

Sadie lifted her hands in a gesture of surrender. "Okay, well, I didn't mean it to be an obscenity. It was in the heat of the moment. I'm sorry, Beth."

"I forgive you," said Beth. "I understand."

"Well, I don't," said Mrs. Olsen. "Two of you were screaming at each other, which I somehow didn't hear from outside, so either this barn has amazing soundproofing or you started yelling just as I came in, and the other two are standing right next to this intense argument, apparently oblivious, about to rip each other's clothes off. Something isn't adding up here."

Their distraction was failing. And Joan could see the door opening behind Mrs. Olsen. Which could only mean that Veronica, Derek, and Finn were about to enter and Wendy didn't have her barrier up yet.

Mrs. Olsen glanced at Joan and narrowed her eyes. "What are you looking at?" She began to turn around.

Beth took a deep breath and shrilly exhaled her trademark banshee shriek, the same scream that she had uttered at age six, just before their class had been cursed with no voices. The same scream that had peppered their childhoods, as each time Beth Fiorelli became overwhelmed with stress, she emitted this head-splitting, eardrum-mangling, sense-obliterating wail of pure human misery.

Even as she clutched her head, Joan had to admit that it was effective. Mrs. Olsen's attention was riveted, her eyes wide and fixed on Beth.

Wendy's face was twisted in pain, but she stepped slowly back from Mrs. Olsen's peripheral vision and began mouthing something, swaying in a simple back-and-forth dance move. A shimmering wall formed in the air in front of her and then disappeared.

Joan saw the exact moment in which Wendy was cut off from the sound, as her entire face and body relaxed.

Beth must have seen it too and she wound down her scream, even though Joan knew from painful experience that she could go for much longer. The woman had the lung capacity of an opera singer on steroids.

Mrs. Olsen, less used to the scream than the rest of them, remained transfixed for a long moment after Beth finished.

Behind her, Veronica and Wendy were directing Derek and Finn, setting up the spell they had planned as quickly as they could, taking no chances that the barrier would hold up to an actual magical assault by Mrs. Olsen.

Joan's mind raced, trying to decide how best to keep the older witch's focus on the four of them, away from the work at the other end of the barn. Much as she wanted to go back to making out with Brandon, that probably wasn't going to work again.

Just then, Sadie's phone began to ring. That could work.

"Answer it," Joan hissed. "It could be Diana."

Sadie frowned at her. "Diana doesn't have my–"

She cut off as Brandon kicked her in the shin, jerking head in Mrs. Olsen's direction.

"Oh." Sadie glanced at Mrs. Olsen, who was starting to snap out of her scream-induced daze. She pulled the phone out of a side pocket of her bag. "Hey, it is Diana!" she said, in an overly cheery voice.

Joan leaned sideways to see who it really was. Ed. She frowned. He was on look-out duty. If he was calling Sadie, that could only be trouble.

Sadie hit Answer. "Hi, Diana. Are you on your way?"

Beth edged closer to hear the response and Joan and Brandon followed suit.

Mrs. Olsen frowned but didn't make any moves toward them.

"What? Oh, is this some kind of ploy? Cool. Go ahead and say what you gotta say," said Ed's voice, faintly from the phone speaker.

"Yeah, we can hold her for a few more minutes, but please hurry," said Sadie.

"Listen there's a car that's gone past me, back and forth, three times now, and keeps slowing down as they pass the driveway. It might be nothing. It just seems weird, and I thought you'd want to know."

"Yeah, thanks. It would definitely help if you could bring several more witches with you," Sadie replied. "We'll keep an eye out for you."

"Should I just talk some more, so that it seems like you're having a real conversation?" Ed asked.

Mrs. Olsen seemed to have recovered her senses. She took a step toward them.

"No, that's fine. I think we're good," said Sadie.

"Okay, bye," said Ed.

"Bye." Sadie hit End and put her phone away.

There was an awkward pause as Mrs. Olsen stopped, apparently unsure of her next step. The only sound on this side of the invisible wall was the witch's furious breathing, as she stood and stared at them, her fists tightly clenched by her sides, her nostrils flaring.

The four of them stared back at her. Joan forced herself to keep her eyes on Mrs. Olsen and ignore Wendy and Veronica, who were now dancing some kind of cha-cha behind her. If they were already dancing, it would only be a few more minutes....

"Call her back." Mrs. Olsen's voice began low and harsh, then spiraled upward as she continued. "Tell her to stay away. Or I swear to fucking Hecate, goddess of witches, I will add to your curse. I will take away your sense of smell and taste too." The witch was now shouting, spittle flying into the air. "I will send you into a coma for a hundred years, like Sleeping Beauty. I will– I will– I can't think of anything else right now!"

Beth took a step backward, away from her.

Joan reached back and took Beth's hand, tugging her forward once more. They all needed to stand together. She gave her an encouraging smile, which Beth returned.

Squaring her shoulders, Beth stared into Mrs. Olsen's eyes. "Do your worst, lady. You don't scare us."

"Oh, don't I?" Mrs. Olsen lifted her arms, splaying them out to either side above her head. "We'll just see about–" She stopped speaking as she suddenly shrunk two inches. "What is happening to me?"

Mrs. Olsen slapped a hand over her mouth at the sound of her voice, which had emerged as a gruff growl.

"It's working," breathed Sadie, stepping forward.

Joan stared, fascinated, at her former teacher, who had shrunk again and was now down to half her previous height and sprouting greyish fur all over her body. "Why is it going so slowly? All of the other spells we've seen have happened all at once."

"Maybe this one is more advanced or something," Brandon suggested.

"Or maybe it's because we deviated from the original," said Sadie.

"It's definitely working, though," said Beth.

As they watched, Mrs. Olsen shrunk all the way down until her form was hidden inside her collapsed skirt and blouse. Joan leaned over the stall gate to peer down at the pile of clothing.

Then she jumped back with a startled, "Holy fuck!" as a two-foot-long rodent with viciously sharp teeth lunged up at her.

CHAPTER 15

"**D**arn, it's an American badger – they are vicious. Well, at least they're a little bit smaller than the European ones," said Beth, calmly stepping up beside Joan to watch as Mrs. Olsen's new form scrabbled at the base of the stall gate. "I hope we have a plan to get her into that cage," she added, nodding at Mugsy's old cage, which had been stripped of all its multi-leveled hamster mazes to make room for a larger animal. "And preferably before she figures out that badgers can't jump, but they can climb."

Sadie smacked Beth in the arm. "Don't say things like that! We have no idea if she can understand us."

"Yeah," said Brandon. "Veronica and Finn could hear everything when they were frozen before."

Joan looked over at Finn, who was advancing with a large fishing net. "Where did you get that?"

"It was in your garage," they replied, their eyes fixed on the badger. Veronica followed with the cage.

"Okay, when I move in, we are doing some serious purging," said Brandon. "You're basically a year away from being on one of those hoarder TV shows."

"I am not. I need that stuff. That's my good stuff," protested Joan.

"Why? Why would you hold onto a fishing net? Have you ever been fishing in your entire life?" he demanded.

"No. I figured I might need it if we ever turned someone into a badger and had to catch them and shove them into an old hamster cage," she said, pointedly.

"And that's another thing," Brandon continued. "How have you had that cage since fifth grade? You've moved three times since then!"

Finn was now a foot away from the badger. They reached the net out in front of them as far as they could, hovering directly above Mrs. Olsen, who didn't react. Slowly, they lowered it down.

As soon as it touched the badger, she went berserk, thrashing and slashing at the net until the rope was in tatters, and then dashing away, backing herself into a corner, teeth bared.

"Damn!" said Finn.

"My fishing net!" cried Joan. "It's ruined."

"Seriously?" said Brandon. "Again, when have you even used it?"

"It was my grandpa's. Probably."

"Probably?" laughed Sadie. "You don't even know where it came from! You didn't know you had one until Finn just told you that it had been in your garage. I'm with Brandon on this one. You have a problem."

"Do you all maybe want to give me hand?" called Finn. "Now that you're no longer cornered in the stall?"

"Oh, sure." Joan opened the door and led the way out into the main area of the barn. "What do you need us to do?"

"I don't know yet," said Finn. "I was hoping the net would work. I don't have a Plan B."

"How do you feel about drugs?" called out Derek from across the room.

"I'm generally in favor," Finn replied.

He held up a syringe and a tube of liquid. "There are some horse tranquilizers in this cupboard."

"Damn, that's pretty hardcore," said Sadie. "I don't think I'd ever do horse tranquilizers."

"He means for the badger," said Joan. "Right?"

Derek sighed. "Yes. I mean for the badger. We can drug her and then get her into the cage, and by the time she wakes up, hopefully we'll have figured out what to do with her."

Veronica frowned. "Aren't those things really strong? I mean, a horse is a lot bigger than a badger. What if we kill her?"

"Well," said Derek. "Then hopefully the curse would go away."

"Nope!" Beth shook her head vigorously. "I said, specifically, just this morning, that I wasn't going to kill anyone. No murder, no manslaughter, no witch-turned-badgerslaughter. I won't be a party to it, and I won't stand idly by and let it happen. No, no, no, no, no!"

"Agreed," said Veronica. "I want this curse gone as much as you, but not at the expense of my karma."

"Fair enough," said Derek. He pulled a box down from the cupboard and examined it. "Ah, here we are. A dosage guide."

"It can't possibly have badger-sized horses listed," said Wendy.

"No, but it has mini-horses," he said. "We can scale down. How much would you say that badger weighs?"

Joan eyed Mrs. Olsen. "Maybe twenty-five pounds?"

"That's about average for an American badger," said Beth.

"Okay," said Derek. "So for a seventy-five-pound miniature horse, you would use fifty-five milligrams. So, correspondingly..." He pulled his phone out of the pocket of his lab coat.

"Eighteen milligrams," said Joan, absentmindedly, her focus still on Mrs. Olsen's menacing posture, as the badger remained cowered in her corner.

Derek looked up, startled. "Oh. Very good."

"Better go a little bit lighter still," said Veronica. "Just in case. It's like salt. We can always give her more, but we can't give her less."

"Fair enough." Derek measured out a small amount of the drug into the syringe. He handed it to Sadie. "Go ahead."

"Me?" Sadie stood there, holding the needle in the palm of her open hand. "Why am I in charge of badger sedation?"

"You work with needles for a living," Derek pointed out.

"Yeah, with people. Not with badgers. I have kids. I need to be careful for their sake, to not get rabies or something."

"If she didn't have rabies as a human, she doesn't suddenly have it as a badger," said Wendy.

"Great," said Sadie. "You do it, then." She held out her hand to Wendy.

"I don't think that's such a great idea." Wendy stared at the needle but didn't take it. "Because, well, I, um."

"Oh, for crying out loud!" Finn scooped the syringe out of Sadie's hand. "I'll do it."

"Be careful, sweetie," said Veronica.

"I'm not going to get within biting reach. As it happens, I have won a few darts tournaments, remember?" Finn walked slowly toward the badger until they were about six feet away. Mrs. Olsen growled.

"Oh, I can't watch!" Beth covered her face with her hands.

Finn positioned their feet carefully and held up the syringe, taking aim and adjusting the predicted trajectory a couple of times. Joan extended an imaginary line from the needle to the badger. It looked good.

Finn threw the needle.

CHAPTER 16

Joan watched as, seemingly in slow motion, the needle flew toward the badger. Mrs. Olsen hissed in anger and rose up onto her hind legs. The syringe embedded itself into her abdomen, just below her ribcage.

Bellowing in rage, Mrs. Olsen charged toward Finn, no discernable sluggishness affecting her at all.

Without missing a beat, Finn reached to their left and moved the hamster cage directly into Mrs. Olsen's path.

The witch-turned-badger tried to skid to a stop but ended up sliding directly into the cage. In one smooth motion, Finn slammed the door shut and then reached through the bars and depressed the syringe.

Mrs. Olsen swayed and then collapsed.

Finn smiled in satisfaction. "Fixed it."

"You're so clever, sweetie," said Veronica, wrapping her partner in an enthusiastic hug and planting an ardent kiss on their lips.

"Nobody ever kisses me like that," complained Sadie. "Maybe I should start internet dating again."

"Really? Even after what happened with Tony?" Joan raised her eyebrows.

"Good point." Sadie's phone rang again and she pulled it out of her purse. "It's Ed again. I wonder if that car's still stalking him."

"What car?" Veronica frowned. "Put it on speaker."

Sadie answered the phone, hitting the Speaker button. "Hey, what's up?"

"Are you guys just about ready to hit the road? There's another car here, and it just pulled into the driveway."

"Oh, crap," said Joan. "It could be the Sigaros or their realtor showing the farm."

"Or someone Marian called in to back her up," said Wendy, grimly.

"It's going to take us a minute to clean up all the spell stuff," said Sadie into the phone. "Can you stall them?"

"Sure thing, boss," said Ed. He hung up.

"Let's boogie," said Derek.

Everyone froze, staring at him.

"What?" said Sadie, finally.

Derek's lips turned up in a small hesitant smile. "It's something my dad used to say. Look, I'm just trying to loosen up a little bit. Be fun."

"I mean, boogying *is* fun," said Brandon. "No one can deny that."

"You're mocking me," Derek said, sadly.

"Where did this come from?" asked Joan, as she stooped to gather up the badger skull and corresponding eyeballs, stowing them in one of Wendy's tote boxes.

"I don't know, you guys just seemed to like me a lot more when I was stoned," said Derek.

"To be fair, we were also stoned," said Sadie. "So we liked everything more."

"And, well, one reason I was so quick to fly in a few days ago, aside from really wanting to kick this curse, is that I ended a relationship recently. Actually, the relationship was ended on my behalf, I should say. Somewhat unexpectedly." Derek kicked a small pile of some flowery herb, scattering it so it blended in with the hay strewn across the barn floor.

"Is that a fancy way of saying you were dumped?" asked Sadie.

"Yes," said Derek. "And one reason that was cited during the transaction–"

"You mean the dumping," clarified Joan.

"Yes. One thing she said was that I was too stiff and stern. Too serious and focused on my work. And on the curse."

"Damn, dude." Sadie put a hand on Derek's white-coated arm. "That sucks. I wouldn't have given you such a hard time if I'd known."

"You can't change who you are, though," spoke up Beth. "Not for someone else. She's not worth being miserable over. And believe me, if you try to be someone you aren't, you will be miserable. It's better to be alone."

"Perhaps," Derek conceded. "It's one thing to know that intellectually, however, and another to know it emotionally."

"Well, maybe just be yourself, but then every now and again, smoke some weed," suggested Sadie.

He almost smiled. "That sounds like a good compromise."

Joan surveyed the barn. "Is that everything?"

"You should always do one final check," said Beth. "Like in a hotel room."

"Yes, I've always said that about barns," said Sadie. "They're exactly like hotels. Especially if you've been fake kidnapped into them and then turned someone into a badger."

A high, girlish voice floated in from the vicinity of the door. "That's a very specific scenario."

Joan whirled around, half expecting to see a cartoon chipmunk standing behind them. Instead, there in the doorway were two people. One of them was Ed, but that wasn't very comforting, as he was floating about a foot off the floor, slowly spinning like he was on a spit, a terrified expression on his face.

CHAPTER 17

"**E**d!" yelled Sadie, rushing forward.

The woman standing beside him lifted a casual hand, and Sadie scooted backward as though pushed by a mighty wind. She thudded into the back wall of the barn. Finn rushed to help her.

Looking at the newcomer, Joan didn't know whether to laugh or scream. The woman was clearly yet another powerful witch, and she didn't seem to be on their side – so that was bad. But on the other hand, she was scantily clad in a short, pleated leather skirt and a leather tube top, with a sword on her back and her platinum hair piled on top of her head in a beehive hairdo. She looked like a cross between Xena: Warrior Princess and Amy Winehouse.

Before Joan could decide how to react, Wendy stepped forward and said coldly, "Carrie, what are you doing here? Let him go – he's with me."

Carrie? Where had Joan heard that name recently?

"Absolutely not," Carrie retorted in that ridiculous, flutelike voice. "He was sneaking around outside, exhibiting very suspicious behavior. And I'm not so certain that you're up to anything good yourself."

"What are you talking about?" Wendy frowned, her eyes narrowing.

Carrie took a step toward Wendy. "Where's your dear mother? Are these the ones she cursed? The non-magicals?" She practically spat the last word.

Brandon put out an arm to stop Joan from surging forward. She subsided, glaring.

"Do you see Marian here? No. Just let my friend go. This doesn't concern you."

"I am here as a representative of the Council of Matriarchs. I'll decide what concerns me," Carrie trilled.

Joan had had enough. She nudged Brandon aside and stepped forward. "We don't answer to your Council of–"

She broke off as Carrie moved her hand again, this time beckoning. Joan found herself drawn swiftly and inexorably forward until her face was inches from Carrie's. The witch's breath smelled like caramel and peppermint, an oddly jarring combination.

"I was talking to Wendy. You will speak only when spoken to, you non-magical chippy."

That was when Joan remembered where she'd heard the name Carrie. "Ah. You must be Diana's daughter. Actually, I'll speak when I want to. I stood down your mother and Wendy's mother, and I'll stand you down too." As she spoke Joan slowly and surreptitiously drew back her foot, and on the last word, rammed it hard into Carrie's shin.

The witch threw back her head, wailing in pain, her hold loosening as she hopped around, clutching her leg.

Joan stepped back, wriggling her toes a little. That had hurt - she was going to have to invest in some steel-toed boots if she was going to go around kicking witches.

Carrie's spell on Ed dissolved, and he fell abruptly to the floor, his ankle twisting, collapsing into an awkward heap.

Sadie rushed forward to help him up. "Are you okay?"

"Oh, yeah, dandy. I am officially over witches. After all of this is done, I'm sticking with ghosts. None of them ever levitated me. Although they do make the walls bleed, and that's pretty gross, to say nothing of ectoplasm. But I'll take that over levitation any day."

With Sadie's help, Ed limped back toward the others.

Wendy stepped forward. "What does the Council want, Carrie?"

Still rubbing her reddened shin, Carrie stood on one foot, glaring at Joan. "They want Marian. She'll be tried for her crimes against you all. And then she'll be punished accordingly. Locked up for years, I imagine. So, I don't know why you're fighting me over it."

"We're not fighting you over that," said Joan. "We're fighting you because you're a Grade A jackass who levitated Ed and assaulted me and Sadie. But it sounds like we have something you want. We're willing to negotiate."

"I don't negotiate with the non-magical," Carrie snapped. She began moving a hand in a lazy circle and a breeze sprang up, quickly becoming a strong, cold wind as she continued. "And frankly, the Council isn't too keen on all of you non-witches gallivanting around, trying to call on them for assistance, getting spells cast on you–"

Joan found herself stumbling, pushed to the side by the swirling wind. She grabbed hold of a horse stall with one hand and Brandon's arm with the other, linking elbows with him as the magical tempest shoved him past her. Together, they braced themselves against the stall.

"What about me?" Veronica fought her way forward, facing Carrie, her legs wide, holding herself in place. "I'm a witch. Will you negotiate with me?"

"You're a witch?" Carrie scoffed. "You look like a vegan hippy."

"Vegans can't be witches?" Veronica bared her teeth in a grimace with the effort of steeling herself against the wind. "I thought the only qualification was the ability to do magic and some kind of witchy ancestry."

Carrie shifted her hand and the wind stopped.

Joan tumbled to the floor then scrambled back to her feet.

She watched as Carrie extended her hand toward Veronica, palm out, and held it there for a moment, closing her eyes briefly. "You do have power. You seem to be completely untrained. Who is your mother?"

Veronica shrugged. "I don't know."

"Ah. But you know where Marian Olsen is? And you'll turn her over to the Council?"

"I have some terms."

Carrie crossed her arms across her small, leather-clad breasts. "What are they?"

"I want our curse lifted. For all of us. Not just me. Not just my friends. The whole class. Everyone who was cursed by Mrs. Olsen will be uncursed." Veronica paused and waited for Carrie to agree. "That's not optional."

"I'll see what I can do."

"She said it's not optional, Carrie!" Wendy slammed a hand forward, and Carrie was thrown back a couple of paces.

"Ow! What did you do that for?" Carrie rubbed her chest. "The Council could probably lift your precious curse. Whether or not they will is another question."

"It's not precious!" said Veronica. "It's– never mind. I want it lifted. And I want Mrs. Olsen prosecuted to the fullest extent of witch law, as long as that doesn't involve execution or torture."

"That's already going to happen," smirked Carrie. "Everyone on the Oregon Council hates her. And no, we don't kill witches."

"I bet they kill non-witches," Joan muttered.

"Only if they know they'll get away with it," said Brandon.

Veronica took a deep breath. "And finally, I want to be taught how to be a witch. Even though most of you seem like a bunch of horrible harpies. But I still want to learn."

Joan glanced at Finn. Their brow was furrowed. Veronica was right – this was not going to go over well.

"You have some nerve, making these kinds of demands on the Council – I would think you'd want to be on their good side if you're asking for training. But you are a witch and you have the right." She smoothed down her leathers, gathering her dignity about herself like a cloak, which, actually, Joan was surprised she wasn't wearing. It was definitely the kind of outfit that should have come with a cloak. "I will be in touch." She nodded toward Wendy. "I suggest you inform your little posse just who they're dealing with."

And with that, she spun around – really missing the dramatic flair that a cloak would have granted – and stalked out of the barn.

Chapter 18

Wendy sighed. "That was very brave, Veronica. I'm not sure it was smart. But it was brave."

"And you say she's not one of the super-powerful ones?" said Beth.

"No, she's powerful," said Wendy. "She's just not as experienced as the Matriarchs. She will undoubtedly be on the Council when she's older."

"So you're saying Veronica just challenged a bunch of people just like that one, except better at it?" said Finn.

"Basically, yeah," said Wendy.

"What happens next?" asked Brandon.

Wendy shrugged. "Honestly, this is uncharted territory for me too. My best guess is that they'll either be offended, in which case you guys will probably all be killed and Veronica and I will be ostracized, or they'll ignore us, and then we're back to convincing Marian to undo your curse."

"K-killed?" said Beth.

"Come on," said Joan, wearily. "The damage is done. Let's get that damn badger back to my place before she wakes up and makes it eighty-five times harder to transport her."

Veronica took charge. "Ed, you can take the cage back in your car. Sadie, Derek, and Beth – you'll ride with him in case anything goes wrong. Take the rest of the tranquilizers. Joan, Brandon, would you each grab a tote? We're all tired, and it's going to be a longer walk back than it was in, so Finn and I will take turns with them too. Wendy? You're the only one with any knowledge of the Council of Matriarchs – come up with an action plan so we can have a little bit of an edge when that idiot Carrie gets back to us."

Joan stooped and picked up the crate closest to her. It definitely felt heavier than it had on the way over.

Sadie and Ed walked past, each carrying one edge of the large cage with the sleeping badger-witch inside. "See you guys back at the ranch," said Sadie, cheerfully.

"What's she so happy about?" muttered Finn.

Joan shrugged. "I guess just that she gets to ride back in a car, while we're stuck hiking through the damn Serengeti. Let's go." She hefted the tote and slogged toward the door and the overgrown grasslands beyond. Brandon trailed behind her, Finn, Veronica, and Wendy following.

Joan walked beside Brandon, sunk into thought, her mind flitting around and around in circles like Mugsy on her hamster wheel. What was going to happen to them? Was there anything they could do to influence their fate?

After a while, Veronica and Finn's conversation behind her trickled forward to Joan's ears.

"I get that," said Finn. "I really do. But you should have talked to me. This isn't how we work, princess."

"I didn't exactly have time in the moment. Anyway, they're the only witches I know," said Veronica. "Wendy's nice. Maybe there are others."

"Can't Wendy teach you?" said Finn. "Or maybe a witch in California?"

"Wendy's still learning herself. And I don't know any witches in Cali. Sweetie, I really think that training with one of these Matriarchs is my best course. We're just going to have to deal with it."

"It might not even be 'we,'" Finn retorted. "Didn't you hear Wendy? You and she might be the ones who come out of this alive. I'm not a witch. Sadie, Brandon, Joan, Derek, Beth – you put these lives on the line too."

Joan felt a pang of sympathy for Finn. Life and death situation aside, relationships were hard enough without your partner suddenly deciding to go haring off to Oregon to apprentice to someone who would probably be a selfish asshole, at least based on the examples they'd seen so far.

Not that Joan had a lot of experience with actual relationships. She glanced sidelong at Brandon beside her. What would she do if Brandon suddenly decided he wanted to become a ... she tried to think of the worst people she knew.... politician? And she suddenly had to hang out with other politicians? She shuddered.

Finn and Veronica could probably use a break from arguing, and she was getting tired of carrying the tote. "Hey," she called back to them. "You two want to take over here?"

Veronica hurried forward. "Sure thing, sweetie."

"Don't call me that." Joan handed over her tote, and Brandon handed his to Finn.

Wendy jogged forward from the tail end of the group.

"Got any thoughts about how to deal with the Council?" said Brandon.

"Well, most of them are horrible old hags like Diana. Matriarch Parrish is the only one with any kind of sense of humor and compassion. She's our best angle, and I know her grand-daughter. I just texted her, and apparently, Matriarch Parrish was recently voted Speaker of the Council. So that's good news. I had Adrian call her grandma, though, and she says right now they're split right down the middle on whether to lift your curse, which is better than I thought. They're actually considering it; apparently, even more than getting their hands on Marian, they're very interested in training Veronica. And more good news – only a few of them want to kill you."

"Oh, good," said Finn. "We're saved."

Veronica frowned at them.

"Down the middle?" said Brandon. "Why? Why not make a goodwill gesture, if she thinks they'll be willing to let us go free anyway?"

"Apparently, lifting your curse sets a bad precedent or something. The argument is that if they lift this curse, then anyone else who's been cursed is going to come clamoring at them to lift theirs too, and it's going to create too much work for them going forward."

"How many witches are going around cursing people?" asked Finn.

"More than should be, I guess," said Wendy. "Adrian doesn't think I'll have any real influence here, because I'm a pretty unknown witch, raised by mages, and connected so closely to Marian."

"Okay, so what happens now?" asked Joan. She couldn't help but notice that the group as a whole seemed to be in deep denial about the possibility of imminent death. Probably for the best.

"I'm not sure. I guess we keep waiting for word from Carrie. And Veronica, you'd better take point on the negotiations."

Joan sighed and turned back in the direction of her house. "So, really, nothing's changed."

"That's not true," said Finn. "Now we know that there's about a 50/50 chance this didn't work."

Veronica frowned at her partner. "And an equal chance that it did! To say nothing of the lower odds of death to all! Let's look on the bright side, sweetie."

One corner of Finn's mouth lifted in a sour half-smile. "That's your job, Princess. I've never been as good at it."

"Fine." Veronica sighed. "Just mope around then." She stalked forward, lugging her tote at her hip.

Joan smiled awkwardly at Finn. "You want to walk with us? You can be as negative as you need to be."

"Thanks. I'd better sort this out, though." Finn hurried to match speed with Veronica.

"They'll be okay, right?" said Joan, staring after Finn and Veronica.

"Of course," said Brandon. "That there is the Golden Relationship, upon which all other relationships are based. Years from now, when we are old and bickering and don't know how to reconcile, we'll still be saying, 'What would Finn and Veronica do?'"

She grinned at him. "Us? Old and bickering? More like old and snuggling. We'll be the best couple and blow those amateurs out of the water."

He smiled and wrapped an arm around her waist, pulling her close against him as they walked. "You're absolutely right, my love."

"'My love,'" she repeated. "I like that one. You may call me that."

Brandon leaned back to look at her. "Really?"

"Yeah. It's nice. And it's not condescending. I'm your love, you're my love. We're all lovey-dovey together. I approve."

"Mmm. Excellent."

Finally, they reached Joan's house. Joan set her tote down on the patio table and collapsed into a metal mesh chair with a sigh. "I need about ninety hours of sleep."

Wendy's phone rang, and Joan pulled herself upright as Wendy glanced at it.

"Who is it?" asked Finn.

Wendy looked up, her face tense. "It's Diana. They must have made some kind of decision."

"Is it a good sign or a bad sign that they decided so quickly?" asked Joan.

Wendy shook her head. "I have no idea."

"Oh, for crying out loud, just–" Veronica stepped forward and grabbed the phone out of Wendy's hand and hit the Answer button. "Hello?"

A tinny mumble emerged from the phone, and Wendy reached forward and hit Speaker. Diana's strident voice boomed forth. "–on this complicated matter. Don't you agree, Wendy?"

Wendy cleared her throat. "Um. Could you repeat the question, please?"

There was a pause. When Diana responded, her voice was full of ice. "I asked if you agreed that it would be best to keep this matter between witches and leave these new naive non-magical so-called friends of yours out of it."

"We've been in it since we were six years old!" exclaimed Veronica.

Joan could almost hear Diana's lips pursing.

"Am I to understand that I am on speakerphone, Wendy?"

"Yes, Diana," said Wendy.

"As I am acting in my capacity as Matriarch and not as your employer, you will address me as such, please."

Wendy rolled her eyes. "Yes, Matriarch Peregrine."

Brandon nudged Joan. "That makes her sound like a headmistress in some kind of horrible old-fashioned boarding school," he muttered.

Joan snickered.

"I heard that," Diana snapped. "I suggest you idiots keep a civil tongue in your heads if you'd like us to remove your curse."

"You realize that's exactly what a headmistress would say, right?" said Finn.

Wendy gestured frantically to them to pipe down. "Sorry, Matriarch Peregrine. I think we're just all a little bit stressed out." She raised her eyebrows and glared around at her friends, drawing a finger pointedly across her throat.

"Yes, sorry," they chorused, reluctantly.

"It's just like you said," added Finn with a pointed look at Veronica. "We're just a bunch of non-magical idiots and only magic really makes anyone worth anything."

Veronica made a face at them. "That's not what I'm saying," she hissed.

Wendy shook her head at them and hit the mute button on the phone. "Not now," she whispered. "We need to present a united front."

She unmuted the phone and Diana's voice emerged again. "Isn't that right, dear?"

Wendy grimaced. "Oh. Um. Sorry, Matriarch Peregrine, I guess I missed the first part of what you said again."

Diana sighed. "You know what? That's it. Consider yourself officially summoned before the Council. And all of your little friends too. You've dragged them in and now you'll all have to face the music. Tomorrow morning. Ten o'clock sharp. If you're late, there will be consequences. Even for you, Wendy."

CHAPTER 19

Joan passed yet another restless night, her dreams a kaleidoscope of first grade, badgers, and bitchy leather-clad chipmunk warriors swinging swords at her and her friends. Finally, at four o'six, she found herself lying in bed, wide awake, staring forlornly at her bedside clock.

She flipped over onto her other side and stared at Brandon for a few minutes. He was sleeping peacefully, a small smile on his face.

"Bastard," she muttered. She watched him for another minute and then slowly reached out her hand toward his face. She braced her middle finger against her thumb and lightly flicked it against his forehead.

Brandon woke up with a sputter. "What? What's happening? What just happened?"

"Oops," said Joan, innocently. "Did I wake you up?"

"I guess so." He rubbed his eyes blurrily and then reached over for his glasses, fumbling as he put them on. "What time is it?"

"Seven," Joan lied. "Time to get up."

"Why does your clock say four o'seven?" Brandon raised an eyebrow at her.

"It's fast. Or slow, I mean."

He grinned. "Your story is starting to unravel, my love."

Joan returned his smile. "I don't know what you're talking about."

"Why is it still dark outside, then?" Brandon fixed her in a mock glare, and Joan's grin widened.

"Daylight savings?"

"Uh-huh." He scooted himself up into a seated position and leaned back against the tall wooden headboard of her antique sleigh bed. "The least you could have done is waited until you'd made coffee before waking me up."

"Sorry. Misery loves company."

"Yeah, well, company loves caffeine," he retorted.

"You're right. Let's go make some coffee," she conceded, throwing the covers off and standing up to stretch.

The hardwood floors were chilly against her bare feet, so she paused to grab her slippers, dislodging her cat, Friday, who was using them as a bed. "Sorry, kitty," she murmured. Friday sauntered off as though it had been her idea to get up the whole time, tail in the air.

Joan wrapped a sweater over her blue tank top and cloud-decorated pajama pants and cracked the bedroom door, listening for any sign of other early risers. The room was quiet except for a faint snore coming from the living room.

She turned to beckon to Brandon and jumped when she found him right behind her, peering over her shoulder.

"Who is snoring?" he whispered.

"Derek, maybe?" she responded. "There's too many people here to know for sure."

"Hopefully they can all go away after today."

"Yes!" Joan began to creep down the hallway, fantasizing about the moment when all of these people – fond as she had become of them – would just go away and leave her and Brandon in peace.

She stopped short in the doorway from the hall to the living room.

Brandon ran into her. "What's going – Oh, wow."

They stared in surprise at the air mattress on the floor. When they'd gone to bed, Derek had been on the couch, Beth curled up on an armchair, and Wendy on the air mattress – alone. Now the three of them were all snuggled up together on the twin mattress like puppies. The snore was coming from Beth.

"Are they dressed?" whispered Brandon.

Joan choked on a laugh and pointed to Derek's arm, still encased in the sleeve of his lab coat, which was the only limb hanging out of the nest of blankets covering the sleeping trio. "Come on. They look too comfy to disturb."

As Joan and Brandon tiptoed past, Derek turned over in his sleep with a snort and threw his arm over Beth. She snuggled closer, her snoring easing a little and then starting back up again.

Once in the kitchen, Joan's autopilot took over. She made a beeline for the coffee maker, opening up the cupboard above it and pulling down the bag of beans. She paused, bag poised over the grinder, thinking about her friends sleeping so peacefully in the next room.

She put the whole beans away and opened up the freezer, shoving aside a stack of microwavable lasagnas to find the pre-ground light roast her dad insisted she keep on hand for him.

Brandon silently handed her two butter knives and she used one as a mallet to chisel away at the frozen grounds with the other. After a couple of hits, a good-sized chunk fell away. Joan held it up next to a measuring cup. Yeah, that looked about right. She loaded it into the coffee maker, saw that Brandon had already filled the reservoir, and hit Start.

The coffee pot began to gurgle. As the drip started and the lovely scent of the coffee began to fill the kitchen, Joan's mind drifted back to the scene in the living room. She frowned. Something was off. What was it?

Joan pictured the room again. All of the furniture had been in place, except for the coffee table, which they'd shoved to the side to make room for the air mattress. The cage sat on top of the coffee table, with a blanket over it–

That was it. The cage's cover had been askew.

Joan whirled around and sprinted back into the living room. She stopped in the doorway and stared at the cage. The blanket had slipped back, and the inside of the cage was visible.

The inside of the empty cage.

CHAPTER 20

"Oh, shit," said Brandon behind her.

Wendy sat up and stretched. "What's going on?" Joan pointed to the cage.

"Oh, shit," Wendy echoed. She nudged Beth and Derek.

Beth rolled over, smacked Wendy in the face, and recommenced snoring.

Derek pulled himself to his feet, tugging down his lab coat, clearly struggling to regain his sense of dignity. "What's going on?" he asked, stiffly. "I must have fallen from the sofa."

"That's the least of our worries," said Joan. "The badger is gone."

At that, Beth bolted awake and into a seated position. "What did you say?" She leaped to her feet and strode over to the coffee table, bending down to peer into the cage. "That's impossible. We gave her another shot of ketamine before we went to sleep. She should still be zonked out."

"And the door is still closed," Wendy pointed out. "There's something weird going on."

"What a surprise," muttered Joan. "I need that coffee before I can deal with this." She marched back into the kitchen, trailed by Brandon, Wendy, and Derek.

"I don't suppose you've also made tea?" Derek inquired.

"Sorry, dude," said Joan. "I didn't think I'd be rousing the household." She grabbed the kettle off the stove and tossed it to him. He caught it deftly.

As Derek filled the kettle at the sink, Joan poured four cups of coffee. She wrapped her hands around her favorite mug, depicting a tornado full of beach chairs, with the caption, *Those bastards on the news said it would be sunny.* She took a sip and felt instantly better. Ahhh, addictions.

Joan grabbed the only unclaimed mug, a purple monstrosity with a picture of Friday on it, a gift from her stepmother, who thought Joan was some kind of crazy cat lady. Joan secretly loved the mug, but would never admit it. She brought it out to Beth, who was still examining the cage in the living room.

Wendy and Brandon followed.

"Thanks." Beth stood up and accepted the coffee. "I'm sorry about this."

Joan frowned, puzzled. "About what?"

"About Mrs. Olsen escaping. I'm the one who knows about animals. I should have taken more steps to prevent it. I feel just awful."

"That's silly," said Wendy. "For one thing, you're a zoologist, not a vet. There's no way you could have known the exact amount of horse tranquilizer to give an American badger. And for another, Marian isn't a regular American badger. There's something else at play here. If anything, I, as the witch of the group, should have–"

"No, no, no!" Beth interrupted. "It's not your fault! You're still learning witchcraft."

Derek's voice floated in from the kitchen. "It doesn't matter whose fault it is. We need to focus on finding and recapturing the badger. We have six hours until we appear before the Council of Matriarchs. And they don't strike me as the types to help us out of the goodness of their hearts."

"He's right," agreed Wendy. "That enchanted badger is our only bargaining chip – the only thing standing between you and those witches. And most of those old hags have no goodness in their hearts at all. The only difference between them and Marian is their fear of being burned at the stake if the world finds out witches are real."

"A not unrational fear," Derek said. "There is certainly precedent for such things." There was a loud clatter from the kitchen and then silence.

Joan raised her eyebrows and met Brandon's eyes. They waited for a moment. "You okay in there?" Joan finally called.

"For the moment." Derek's voice was strained. "I believe I have found the badger."

Joan, Brandon, Beth, and Wendy rushed toward the kitchen, Wendy in the lead. She stopped in the doorway, and Joan crashed into her. Brandon smacked up against her back, and she felt another shove as Beth ran into him. Joan stood on her tiptoes but still couldn't see over the tall witch. She stooped instead, craning her head to see around Wendy's shoulder.

Mrs. Olsen was standing on her hind legs in the doorway of the butler's pantry, her vicious teeth bared. Derek had knocked over the table and was sheltered behind it.

The badger advanced.

"Beth! What do I do?" Derek asked.

"I don't know!" Her voice was panicked. "Do you have any badger balm?"

"Of course not!"

"What the hell is badger balm?" Brandon asked.

"I don't know! I just Googled 'how to soothe a badger,' and that's what came up," said Beth. "Can't you do anything, Wendy?"

"Oh, now you're totally cool with witchcraft?" said Joan.

"I've come around to your way of thinking. I don't want anyone to get mauled by a badger! Anyway, my pastor says we should always be questioning what we've been taught and that the only things that are set in stone are the Ten Commandments and Jesus' love."

"That's very broad-minded of him," said Derek. "But for the love of Jesus, can you guys, for once in your fucking lives, focus!"

The badger took another step toward Derek's table fortress. Derek looked around wildly, then picked up a chair and brandished it toward her, its legs out like swords. "Avast!"

"What's happening out there?" Beth said. "I can't see anything!"

Beth pushed Joan and Brandon slightly to the side. As soon as she could see what was going on, she squealed, and the badger turned in their direction.

"Dammit, Beth!" said Joan.

Mrs. Olsen advanced toward the doorway, and the group took a collective step back into the living room.

Joan picked up The Complete Works of William Shakespeare from the end table where she'd left it the day before. She hefted it in her hand and threw it at the badger's head.

Big mistake.

The badger hissed and lunged straight for her, crossing the room at top speed.

"Hiberent!" Veronica's voice rang out behind Joan.

Mrs. Olsen froze in mid-air, inches from Joan's face, and crashed to the floor, her limbs still outstretched, teeth bared in a snarl.

Joan stood, shaking, staring at the stiff animal in front of her. She felt Brandon's arms wrap around her and allowed him to guide her toward the couch. She looked up at Veronica, who was standing in the doorway, completely naked, hair in disarray.

"What the hell is going on out here?" Veronica demanded. "It's five o'clock in the morning. Why did you let the badger out?"

"We didn't let her out!" Beth's voice was indignant but muffled. She had her arms up over her face, shielding her eyes from Veronica's nudity. "She escaped and attacked us!"

Brandon tossed Veronica a blanket. She caught it and cocked her head at him. "What's this for?"

"I thought you might want to cover up," he said. "What do you have against pajamas?"

"What do you have against the human body?" she retorted.

Derek peeked around the doorway. "Is it safe to come out? Good God, Veronica. Aren't we traumatized enough already?"

She rolled her eyes and wrapped the red blanket around herself. "Fine. But this color looks terrible on me. Also, you're welcome for saving your asses."

"Thank you," said Wendy. "I should have thought of that earlier."

Veronica shrugged gracefully. "That word has been burned into my mind. You were busy being jackfruited in hollandaise when she used it on me and Finn."

"So now what?" said Brandon. "Beth, you can uncover your face."

Beth peeked out from behind her elbows, saw that Veronica was covered by the blanket, and lowered her arms. "I say we take no chances. Keep her under that spell. Give her some more tranks too. Maybe even tie her up and put her back in the cage. And we should all get dressed–" She raised her eyebrows pointedly at Veronica. "And head to Salem now. That way if something happens, we'll have plenty of time to get it all sorted out, and we know we won't be late. This will be the most important day of our lives."

"Agreed," said Derek. "We need to get this one right."

"Is there more coffee?" Veronica asked.

"Put some clothes on first," said Joan. "Then you get coffee."

CHAPTER 21

It was a major undertaking to get Mrs. Olsen back into the cage in her frozen state. Joan, Brandon, and Beth spent about forty-five minutes trying to move her limbs into various poses to get her through the hinged door until finally Finn wandered into the room and pointed out that the top of the cage was removable.

They weren't taking any chances. Mrs. Olsen had somehow gotten out of that cage once before. So Joan dug some twine out of a junk drawer. Beth tied together her front paws, Brandon tied together her back paws, and then Joan dredged out her old Girl Scout knot knowledge and connected the ropes together.

And finally, they wrapped her up in Veronica's blanket and placed the whole badger bundle into the cage. It filled the entire space. Even if she somehow unfroze herself, hopefully she wouldn't be able to move.

Meanwhile, Wendy and Derek filled a duffle bag with everything that could possibly be needed at the Council meeting. Spell components, snacks, a first aid kit, the grimoire, and finally, the skeleton key that Joan had found the week before, which had brought them all together.

Then the group divided up into two cars and drove to Salem, Joan swinging by Sadie's house and Ed's dad's apartment to pick them up on the way.

The Council of Matriarchs turned out to be headquartered in one of those nondescript grey stone downtown buildings that no one ever seems to notice, or if they do, they assume it houses some government agency, full of sad little bureaucrats living sad little bureaucratic lives. There was no signage outside, no statuary or architectural flourishes.

As they mounted the short staircase to the door, Joan noticed a black cat sunning itself off to the side. The cat lifted its head and watched as Brandon tried to pull the handle open.

"Let me try," Wendy suggested. Sure enough, the door opened for the witch. Joan was the last one inside, and she glanced over at the cat before walking in. It was gone.

Inside, the place was anything but non-descript. The word *opulent* drifted into Joan's mind as she looked around, her eyes wide. They found themselves in a huge antechamber floored in marble with thick, vibrantly red rugs scattered around. At one end of the room was a set of enormous, intricately carved dark wood double doors – the kind of doors that you'd expect to find in Middle Earth, leading into an elven palace.

Throughout the room, black leather couches and armchairs had been arranged into several conversation areas. There was a sideboard stocked with coffee, several varieties of tea, and steaming cinnamon rolls. Across from the coffee station was a bar and a wine rack. Brandon wandered over and pulled out a bottle of red. He whistled. "Good taste."

"I guess witches do pretty well for themselves," said Derek.

Brandon opened the fridge beside the bar and brandished a bottle of champagne. "Mimosa, anyone?"

"Yes, please!" Joan sank onto a couch. "Oh, this is nice."

"Isn't it a little early for that?" Beth frowned as she poured herself another cup of coffee. "The sun isn't even up."

"Exactly," said Sadie, busily cutting oranges in half behind the bar. "It's still night time. If anything, we're being responsible by sticking to mimosas instead of breaking out the Scotch."

"An excellent point." Ed looked up from the bookcase he was perusing. "I'll have one too, for sure. After all, we might be dead soon."

Brandon pulled down four flutes from the rack over the bar. "Anyone else?"

"Oh, what the hell," said Finn. "I'm in. Princess? Have some fresh-squeezed OJ, at least."

"In a bit, sweetie." Veronica unrolled the blue yoga mat she had brought in with her. "I need to get some of this tension out of my system first."

"I'll have one," said Derek.

All activity in the room ceased as every head turned to stare at Derek.

"You don't think maybe we should focus on preparing for the meeting?" said Joan.

"And keep a clear head?" asked Sadie, her arm frozen on the lever over her head as she had paused in the middle of juicing an orange.

"Are you okay, sweetie?" Veronica frowned at him. She walked over and placed a hand on his forehead. "You don't feel feverish."

He sighed. "I feel tightly wound and stressed out. One mimosa isn't going to derail my entire brain, is it?"

"How often do you drink?" asked Joan.

"I had a gin and tonic once in grad school."

"Oh, this should be fun," cackled Sadie. "You should definitely have a mimosa."

"Better yet," suggested Ed. "Let's revisit that Scotch idea."

"Ease up off him," said Beth. She had settled into a chair and pulled some knitting out of her purse. "He's a grown man. He can have a mimosa or not, as he pleases."

"How about you?" said Sadie. "You want one?"

"No, thanks," she said, primly. "I will stick with coffee because that is what I please to do."

Brandon shrugged and lined up the champagne flutes. "Okay, five mimosas coming up."

Sadie poured the fresh juice into the flutes as Brandon wrestled with the cork. Finally, it POPPED out of the bottle and he finished up the cocktails and placed them on a tray. Sadie took the tray and distributed the drinks.

As Joan accepted her mimosa, a black cat jumped up into her lap.

"Oh! Hello," she said. "Where did you come from?"

"Wasn't that cat outside on the steps when we came in?" asked Brandon, sitting down beside her.

"It can't be the same one," she said. "It didn't come in with us. And there are no open doors or windows in here. It had to have been inside already."

Joan set down her drink and examined the cat's collar. "Sabrina," she read. "That's a little cliché, isn't it?"

"Maybe she's someone's familiar," suggested Sadie. "Oh, or a witch in disguise! Could she be a witch in disguise, Wendy?"

"Doubt it. She's probably just a pet," said Wendy. "Shapeshifting is pretty hardcore, and I don't think anyone would do it lightly. It's more complicated to do it yourself than like what we did to Marian."

The usually-calm and self-possessed witch was fidgety, keeping the cage holding her mother close to her feet as she sat on the couch across from Joan.

"Are you going to be okay?" Joan asked, concerned. "If you'd rather wait out here, I think we'd all understand. It's got to be rough, standing before a ruling council of your mother's people, arguing to condemn her while making demands on behalf of a group of people you just met a few days ago."

Wendy gave her a grateful smile. "No, really, I'm fine. I feel like I know you guys better than I know her. And you've never turned me into a sleeper agent, so that's about eighty-five points in your favor. Besides, most of them won't bother to negotiate with anyone who isn't a witch and if we're all going to get through this, you'll need every advantage. Even if I'm not in favor, I'm in more than most of you. You need me in there with you."

"Well, thank you, sweetie, for being so supportive of us," said Veronica from her yoga mat, as she smoothly moved from a warrior pose into a downward-facing dog. "You've been a true friend."

Joan was impressed by Veronica's yoga prowess, despite herself. If she'd tried to do the same, she would have ended flat on her ass, out of breath and irritated. She had never found yoga to be quite the calming experience it was supposed to be.

She took a sip of her mimosa, savoring its bubbliness and the sweet flavor of the fresh-squeezed juice. "Oh, this is fantastic," she said. "Fresh-squeezed for the win."

"It's also top-shelf champagne," said Brandon. "I've always made my mimosas with $5 brut. And that's $5 for the magnum from the bulk store. I think this just ruined me for those."

"Nah," said Ed. "Cheap mimosas are still perfect for those random Sundays when you're broke as shit, but you just gotta brunch it up."

"I'll drink to that," said Sadie, leaning forward to clink her glass against his.

"This is a rather interesting set of flavors," observed Derek. "I would never have thought that carbonation and orange juice would compliment each other so perfectly."

"Haven't you ever had orange pop?" asked Finn. "Same concept, but with booze."

"Where are you from, Finn?" Wendy raised an eyebrow. "They don't say 'pop' in California, do they?"

"I'm a corn-fed Iowa kid. Can't you tell?" Finn grinned as they gestured to their slim figure.

"But this is simply extraordinary," said Derek again. "Isn't alcohol meant to taste astringent? This is so sweet." He drained his glass. "I'll have another. For the sake of observation."

Sadie jumped to her feet. "Hurray! Another round!" She tossed back the remainder of her own drink. "Who else?"

Joan shrugged and exchanged a glance with Brandon. They clinked glasses and chugged. Ed drained his as well.

Finn elected to continue sipping. "Someone's gotta keep a clear head."

"My head is clear, sweetie," said Veronica.

"I know, princess, but I want you and me to be on the same page here."

Veronica frowned and inhaled deeply. She moved into a complicated pose that seemed to involve putting one foot behind her ear and the other up in the air while supporting herself on one hand. Joan couldn't even see what the other arm was doing. "Suit yourself, sweetie."

Sadie collected the flutes, almost dropping two of them.

Ed jumped up and unburdened her of half the glasses, following her to the bar to help mix the second round.

Two rounds later, the imposing double doors finally creaked open and a dignified young woman in a black suit emerged.

Sabrina the cat, who had been lying on her back on Joan's lap getting belly rubs, jumped onto the floor and proceeded toward the woman, twining between her ankles before sauntering into the dimly lit cavern beyond.

"You are the penitents?" she asked.

"I guess so," said Joan.

Derek stood up and tripped over his feet. He giggled madly and then made a visible effort to compose his face into its usual stern expression. "We're not penitents," he said, "we are here to bargain. We present a strong, united front. We have the badger, you know."

The woman raised an eyebrow. "The . . . badger?"

Wendy stepped forward. "Yes."

The woman turned to face Wendy. "Yes, you are penitents or yes, you have a badger?"

Wendy shrugged. "Both."

"Very well. Follow me." She turned and led the way into a narrow corridor, not waiting to see if they were following.

The seven of them trooped in, Derek staggering a little and still clutching his mimosa. Wendy caught hold of his arm to steady him.

Joan felt a little bit light-headed herself. She grabbed Brandon's hand for moral and physical support, and he squeezed hers back. She saw Veronica and Finn holding onto each other's hands in front of her. Then she glanced back and noticed that Sadie and Ed were walking very close together too. Beth brought up the rear with no one to lean on, her head held high. Maybe she was holding onto Jesus' hand. Joan suppressed a giggle.

Then they rounded the corner into the actual Chamber and her laugh died in her throat. The room was huge. And scary.

The ceiling had to have been thirty feet up, and the Matriarchs were seated on a high dais, towering a good fifteen feet above the floor, staring down at them like insects.

Joan narrowed her eyes. So that's how they wanted to play it? They thought they could intimidate her? Screw 'em. She dropped Brandon's hand and stepped forward, scanning the thirteen faces above her head until she found Diana. She glared directly into the older witch's eyes. "Afraid to face us on the same level? You gotta resort to cheap tricks?"

"Silence!" snapped their guide. "You will address the Matriarchs with respect."

Joan snorted. "I respect people who treat others with common fucking decency."

A witch in the middle of the tribunal pounded on the table in front of her with a gavel. Joan turned her attention to the new woman and noticed with interest that this one looked like she was fighting back a grin. This one had to be Matriarch Parrish, the Council Speaker.

The Matriarch spoke in a rich, humor-filled voice. "I think we're getting off to an unnecessarily rocky start here. Let's begin again. I believe we are essentially here to negotiate with one Veronica Grinner, yes? Which of you is Veronica?"

Veronica stepped forward. She put her hands together in a prayer pose and gave a small bow. "I'm Veronica, your honor."

The witch laughed. "The proper address is Matriarch, but 'your honor' is very nice too. I understand that you have Marian Olsen in your custody and are willing to exchange her for a promise that she be prosecuted to the fullest extent of our law and the removal of a certain curse from yourself and your former classmates. Is this correct?"

Veronica nodded.

"And additionally, you wish to enter the sisterhood of witches as a student?"

With a sideways glance at Finn, who stood with their lips pursed, Veronica nodded again. "Yes, Matriarch."

Diana leaned forward. "And where is Marian Olsen?"

"Oh, no," said Sadie, wagging a finger. "We weren't born yesterday. We tell you where the hostage is after you agree to our terms!"

"You have not been addressed, girl," admonished another witch, a sour-faced hag who was ninety if she was a day, and by the looks of it hadn't smiled once in all those ninety years.

"Neither have you, bitch," retorted Derek.

Beth gasped and it echoed in the chamber as everyone stared at him.

The sour-faced witch stood, leaning on a cane. "What did you say?"

"He said nothing, Matriarch Miller," said Wendy, quickly. "He didn't mean it."

The Matriarch turned her formidable glare to Wendy. "Ms. Olsen, isn't it?"

Wendy hesitated. "It's Sharp, Matriarch."

"You dare to come into our presence and claim the name of your father? And a mage, at that? And did you think that this would ingratiate you to us? We are witches, young lady."

"Well, Matriarch, seeing as how my mother is about to be locked up for cursing thirty ordinary children, I don't think using her name is all that much better."

Joan held her breath as Matriarch Miller studied Wendy for a long moment before nodding curtly and taking a seat once again. "Fair enough. See that you keep your gang in line."

"Can we return to the matter at hand?" Diana said. "I see no proof that you have any way to hand Marian Olsen over to us at all. She isn't here, that much is clear. So we seem to be at an impasse. You don't trust us enough to tell us and we certainly don't trust you."

"Don't you see? How can you be so stupid?" said Derek. "We have Mrs. Olsen right here!"

And before anyone could stop him, he shoved the cage forward with his foot.

Chapter 22

The Council stared at the cage. Joan glanced at it too. The badger was so bundled up that it appeared to be just a red blanket filling a wire cage.

"Oh, I shouldn't have done that," said Derek into the silence. "There's nothing in the cage. Nothing at all. Just a blanket. Definitely not a badger."

Matriarch Parrish gestured to the woman who had ushered them in. "Sylvia, will you please open that cage?"

"I would be delighted, Matriarch," said Sylvia, solemnly.

Joan very much doubted that Sylvia ever indulged in anything like delight. Then again, if Derek was standing in front of her, drunk off his ass from three mimosas, anything was possible.

Sylvia knelt and unhooked the cage door. As she struggled to pull the blanket through the small opening, Veronica stepped forward again, taking a deep breath.

"Matriarchs, I implore you to hear our case. Twenty-nine years ago, we were cursed. We were children – ordinary, non-magical children, suddenly touched by your world. We never asked to be made aware of the existence of witches. But here we are. And there are more of us. On that day, when we were kids, our experience was dismissed as a mass hallucination. Children are almost always dismissed. But we're adults now. And in a few months, this curse will come back. And all of these adults will find themselves without voice or sight. But we'll still have internet connections. And I guarantee you the existence of witches will be made known. Alongside the location of this building and the names of every member of this Council and all of your daughters."

She stepped back and crossed her arms.

Diana grinned at her. "I like you. You've got as much spirit as this one–" she nodded toward Joan, "–but you've got power too. You have my vote."

"You do not have mine," snapped Matriarch Miller. "I do not take threats lightly. What's to stop us from simply killing all of you?"

"You can kill the seven of us," said Finn, stepping forward and taking Veronica's hand in theirs.

"I didn't agree to that," interrupted Ed.

Finn directed a brief glare in his direction before continuing. "But I've been recording this on my phone and I set a certain social media site to collect the audio and post it in one hour. Agree to our terms and I can cancel the scheduled post. Kill us, and it's already in the cloud."

"And the rest of our class has already been emailed the location of this building and your witch shop," said Beth. "Are you prepared to hunt them down and kill all of them?"

"Perhaps," said another witch. "Are you prepared to risk our wrath on their behalf?"

"I'm prepared to suspect that you aren't willing to risk the police investigation," she retorted.

"What is your vote, then, Matriarch Rivers?" asked Matriarch Parrish.

The witch leaned forward and studied Beth for a moment. "Aye. I'll vote in their favor." She sat back and crossed her arms, her eyes still locked on Beth, whose lips twitched in a satisfied smile. The witch nodded her grudging respect.

"We now have two in favor and one against," said Matriarch Parrish. "Matriarch Praskovitch. How do you vote?"

An iron-haired horse-faced woman seated at one end stood. "Strongly against. I recommend immediate termination. I'm calling their bluff." She sat down.

Joan wondered if it was a bluff. Had Beth actually had the foresight to email the class all of that information?

"Very well. Your recommendation is noted." Matriarch Parrish moved down the line. "Matriarch Keystone?"

"Oh, what the hell, let's help the poor bastards out. I vote in favor."

"Matriarch Jones?"

"Aye. If only to bring this Veronica into our fold."

"Matriarch Collins?"

"Nay. Would they do the same for us? I think not." The Matriarch frowned down at the group of penitents.

"What does that even mean?" muttered Joan. "How would we lift a curse from them?"

Brandon squeezed her hand and shook his head. "Some people are just contrary. It's tied now," he murmured.

"Matriarch Hausen?"

"It's no skin off my nose. Aye."

They were back in the lead.

"Matriarch Albens?"

"Absolutely not. Where does it end?" The witch looked down her long nose at them.

"Matriarch Takata?"

"Aye. And I'll throw in my hat for Veronica's apprenticeship."

Tied again.

"Matriarch Muldoon?"

A blousy witch with bright red-dyed hair frowned at them. She shook her head. "No. I can't be bothered with this nonsense. Off with their heads and wash our hands of the whole damn thing."

Now there was just one more, plus Matriarch Parrish. Joan was pretty sure Matriarch Parrish was going to vote in their favor. She eyed the only other Matriarch who had yet to vote. This didn't look promising. The woman's eyes were narrowed, her lips pursed, and her posture was far too straight. She rubbed her neck, wondering how many votes would be needed for the worst-case scenario.

"Matriarch McKinley?"

This last Matriarch took her time. She studied the group intently, her gaze lingering on Veronica. "You!" She gestured abruptly toward Veronica, who stepped forward.

"Yes, Matriarch?" Veronica's voice was even and measured.

"Who is your mother? How is it that you are only now beginning to learn witchcraft?"

"I don't know," Veronica answered. "I was taken away from her by social services when I was a baby. My adopted family has always been enough for me."

The Matriarchs muttered among themselves. Matriarch McKinley remained silent, staring straight through Veronica. The yogi simply gazed back, apparently unfazed.

Finally, Matriarch McKinley rose to her feet, her eyes never leaving Veronica's face. "Aye. I vote in favor of the petition."

Matriarch Parrish's gavel hit the desk once more. "As do I. Congratulations – your request has been granted."

Diana leaned forward. "Sylvia, how are you coming with that cage?"

Joan glanced down at Sylvia, who had managed to extract a corner of the blanket and was tugging at it, her lips pursed in frustration.

Finn stepped forward and deftly opened up the top of the cage, lifting out the blanket. They unrolled it to reveal the stiff figure of Mrs. Olsen's badger form. "Wendy and Veronica turned her into a badger. Then Veronica froze her in place."

"Very nice." Matriarch McKinley nodded her approval as Diana emitted a bark of laughter.

"Sylvia, you may return the accused to her cage and take her out to the holding cell. We'll deal with her later," ordered Matriarch Parrish.

Sylvia bowed and took the badger back from Finn, carefully re-wrapping her in the blanket and then leaving through a small door next to the dais. A moment later, a new, identically-dressed woman, considerably older, replaced her beside the penitents.

"And now for your curse," said Diana. "Do you have the focal object?"

Wendy reached into her duffel bag, extracting the skeleton key from a side pocket. "I believe this is it, Matriarch Peregrine."

"Sabrina? Bring me that key, please," said Matriarch Parrish.

Joan eyed the new attendant nervously as Wendy handed over the key. Sabrina? Was this really the cat she'd been petting earlier? The black-haired, green-eyed woman – there was something odd about those eyes – smiled briefly at Joan before turning toward the tribunal and climbing a small ladder to the side of the dais. She passed the key to Matriarch Praskovitch at the end of the table, who examined it.

"Interesting," she remarked. "This object is completely suffused with bitter hatred. It's a little unpleasant."

"Imagine going through life thinking that bitter hatred is only a little unpleasant," muttered Sadie.

"I feel like that one has placed a couple of curses in her day too," murmured Joan.

"What was that?" Matriarch Praskovitch pinned Joan in a narrow-eyed stare.

"Nothing, ma'am." Joan fought to keep a straight face. The last thing they needed now was one of the witches who'd been on the fence to change her vote on this old hag's behalf.

"Uh-huh." Raising an eyebrow, Matriarch Praskovitch continued. "I assume you know the words of the original curse?"

Beth stepped forward and recited:

"I have your attention right now,

And I'll keep it awhile, I vow.

In one score and ten,

I will see you again.

To silence and darkness you'll bow."

Matriarch Rivers leaned forward. "Is that a limerick?"

"Yes," said Veronica. "We've had fights that lasted for years, debating over whether the limerick form was necessary for a curse or if Mrs. Olsen just had a weird sense of whimsy."

"It is not needed," said Diana. "But it's pretty impressive that she came up with it on the spot."

"No matter," said Matriarch Parrish. "We'll need to get her into her counter-mood. How do we make a badger happy? Some kind of badger treat?"

"Do you have any badger balm?" asked Beth.

"No one even knows what that is," said Ed. "There's no way they have any."

"Actually," Sabrina spoke up. "I believe we do have some, left over from that unpleasantness in the garden last year."

"You had a badger in your garden?" said Beth. "In the middle of a city? In Oregon?"

"No," said Sabrina. There was an awkward silence, but apparently, she didn't feel the need to expand on that.

"Oh," said Beth after a moment. "Okay. But you've got the balm?"

"Yes."

"Please go and get it, Sabrina, and see if you can get Marian into the proper state of mind and draw some blood," said Matriarch Parrish. Sabrina nodded once and sauntered away.

"You'll have to excuse her," said Matriarch Rivers. "You know how cats get when they get older. She just doesn't give a fuck about anything anymore."

"So she is a cat?" said Joan.

"Yes, they make wonderful attendants, if a little unpredictable," said Matriarch Parrish. "Veronica, if you would remain here, we would like to chat with you. The rest of you can adjourn back to the waiting area."

Veronica reached her hand out to grasp Finn's again. "Finn stays too."

Matriarch Parrish shrugged. "Suit yourself." She rang a little bell and yet another black-suited woman, this one barely more than a teenager, bounced into the chamber.

Joan looked at her closely and could see that her ears were slightly pointed and her pupils slitted. Her hair was brown with white streaks. The young woman led them back out into the antechamber and then sat down on a couch in a corner.

Brandon pulled Joan back to the same sofa they'd been sitting on before. Their glasses were still there, and they'd been refilled. As she picked up her mimosa, Joan glanced back over at the attendant and saw a brown tabby cat cleaning her paws where the woman had been sitting.

Wendy sat down heavily across from Joan. "This seems like it could be a while. I think it's going to take more than badger balm to make Marian happy."

"She has had a rough couple of days," Sadie snickered.

Derek laid down next to Wendy, putting his head in her lap. "Wendy, has anyone ever told you that you have the comfiest lap?"

Wendy grinned. "No, Drunk Derek, I can't say that anyone ever has."

"Maybe you should get some sleep, Drunk Derek," suggested Sadie.

Wendy stroked his black hair. "You've had a rough couple of days, too."

"Thank you, guys! I have had a tough time of it." He closed his eyes. "Will you sing me a lullaby?"

"I don't think I know any," said Wendy.

Beth, seated on the couch directly behind them, began to sing softly as she knitted. *"Down in the valley...."*

Sadie joined in, her smooth alto a beautiful counterpart to Beth's soft soprano. *"The valley so low...."*

Brandon and Ed joined in, harmonizing with their tenor voices. *"Hang your head over. Hear the wind blow."*

Joan leaned back on the couch and closed her own eyes, letting the old folk song wash over her. She opened her eyes again as the tabby cat jumped into her lap, adding a low purr to the lullaby. Joan absent-mindedly stroked the cat's ears.

A quiet snore floated toward her. Glancing across the coffee table, she saw that Derek was fast asleep, his head still on Wendy's lap. Wendy met her eyes and shrugged, a rueful smile on her lips.

"Hear the wind blow." The impromptu choir wrapped up their song, and Joan silently clapped her hands in appreciation.

"That was really gorgeous, you guys," said Wendy.

Joan nudged Brandon. "How come you never sing for me like that?"

He slung his arm around her. "Well, you–"

Abruptly, Joan's body was wracked by an intense jolt of electricity – far more extreme than when she'd been cursed or when she'd seen the key for the first time. She sat, rigid, unable to move, her entire being stricken.

And just as quickly, it was over. Joan found herself fallen to the floor, gasping for breath, every muscle in her body aching. After a moment, finally able to breathe, she lifted her head and saw that Brandon, Sadie, and Ed lay beside her in similar states. Derek was still on the couch, but he was curled into a ball, whimpering.

Wendy's eyes were wide and wild, her arms wrapped around Derek protectively.

"What's going on?" she demanded. "Are you okay?"

With effort, Joan pushed herself into a seated position, leaning against the edge of the couch. "I think our curse might be gone."

Beth crawled around the couch she had been sitting on. "I feel a weird empty spot in my soul that I never noticed was clogged."

"It feels wonderful," said Sadie. "I mean, not physically. Physically, I feel like shit. Like I just ran a marathon that I was so not prepared for."

"Yeah," said Joan. "But on the inside–"

"We're cured," said Brandon.

"Well, that was fast," said Ed. "I wonder how they managed to get Mrs. Olsen into a happy state of mind."

"We turned her back into a woman and hypnotized her," said Matriarch Parrish from behind them.

Joan snapped her head around. "Where the hell did you come from?"

Matriarch Parrish smiled enigmatically. "That would be telling. And, yes, you are now free of your curse. You don't need to worry about it coming back or about Marian Olsen coming after you. Nor will the Council pursue you or your classmates, provided there is no trouble from you. You may go and never come back. Except you, Wendy. You may come back."

"What about Veronica and Finn?" demanded Sadie.

"That is not my story to tell," she said. "But I believe it will be an interesting one."

"Are they coming back with us?" asked Beth.

Matriarch Parrish shook her head. "Veronica has been assigned to a Matriarch for schooling and she and her partner will be staying here for the foreseeable future."

"What about their dog?" asked Sadie. "Can I drop her off later?"

The tabby cat jumped down from the couch and hissed.

"We don't do dogs here," said Matriarch Parrish, firmly.

"Great." Sadie threw up her hands. "So now she's my problem?"

"Have some perspective," Matriarch Parrish suggested. "Instead of being cursed to be blind and mute, you get a cuddly friend. Now. It is time for you to leave."

Matriarch Parrish clapped her hands briskly.

And Joan found herself outside, standing at the top of the stone stairs, Brandon, Sadie, Ed, Derek, Beth, and Wendy beside her, Sabrina the black cat sunning herself on the top step in front of them.

"That's that," said Wendy. "Let's go."

Epilogue

Joan sat on her back patio that evening and closed her eyes, reveling once again in the tranquil silence of her rural home, disturbed only by birdsong and crickets. She could almost taste the solitude.

Beth had gone back to her own house, a couple towns over, and Ed was on his way back up to Seattle. Wendy had agreed to let Derek stay with her until he was ready to go back to England – he had already arranged a six-month sabbatical from his lab, so he had decided to take some time and figure out how his life would be now that the curse, his main purpose in life, was gone. Veronica and Finn's stuff was still in the guest room, but they were presumably still in Salem, and who knew when they'd be back. For now, all that mattered was that they weren't here.

The back door opened and Brandon walked out, balancing two martini glasses, a large shaker full of ice, two liquor bottles, and a jar of olives on a tray. "Ready?" he asked, setting it down on the glass tabletop.

"I was born ready," she said.

"Really?" he raised an eyebrow. "Typically babies don't start drinking martinis right when they're born."

"Okay, well, I was born to be ready right now, then."

Brandon grinned. "Let's get our martini on." He poured two double shots of a locally distilled gin and then two shots of dry vermouth into the shaker, topping it off with a splash of olive juice. He stirred it with a spiral-handled bar spoon and strained the liquid into the glasses, dividing it evenly. Two olives plopped into each drink.

"The perfect martini," said Joan, carefully lifting her glass. "What are we toasting?"

"To never having to interact with witches again," suggested Brandon.

"Not even Wendy? Or Veronica?" Joan shook her head. "At the very least, Veronica needs to come by and get her stuff out of my guest room at some point."

"Our guest room," Brandon corrected with a grin.

Joan returned the goofy smile. "Of course."

"I've got it." Brandon lifted his glass and clinked it against hers. "To us, my love."

"Fuck, yes. To us." Joan sipped her martini. "Perfect."

Author's Note:

You've officially made it through **three books of the *Rhymes With Witch* series**, and I appreciate you more than you know.

If you're wondering what happens next — good news. The next arc of *Rhymes With Witch* is in progress, following Veronica and Finn into their next chapter. Expect more magical chaos, questionable life choices, and the kind of small-town weirdness that refuses to stay small.

Stay tuned.

If you'd like to keep reading in the meantime, all of my other series take place in the same magical world — just with very different vibes.

In the mood for slightly higher stakes (with plenty of humor)?

Try the **Mathilda Holiday** series. It follows two sisters targeted by an ancient secret society.

Start with Book 1 here:

Ready for something darker and more intense?

Try **Warrior Mage Librarians** — a high-stakes fantasy series about a soft-hearted scholar and a battle-hardened warrior nun who find themselves at the center of a global cryptid war.

Start with *Blood Falls* here:

And even if this is where you pause for now, thank you for reading *Rhymes With Witch*. I hope to see you again whenever you're ready for your next adventure. — Anna

About the Author

Anna McCluskey is an Oregon-based, semi-nomadic, almost-entirely-feral fantasy author.

Anna is the author of the *Mathilda Holiday* series, the *Rhymes With Witch* series, the *Warrior Mage Librarians* series, and the upcoming stand-alone anthology *The Bloody Unicorn and Other Delightfully Dark Drinks*.

She has had several poems published in journals and anthologies, and her short fiction has been read by at least a dozen people, many of whom murmured appreciatively about it.

For information on upcoming projects and general merriment, check out her website, www.annamccluskey.com.